Rupert's Diary

MARILYN SAUNDERS

Published 2019 by Shadenet Publishing
www.shadenetpublishing.co.uk

ISBN: 978-0-9933040-6-4

Cover designed by Christine Hammacott
https://artofcomms.co.uk/

Also available as an e-book.

For Rupert…

Acknowledgements

Many thanks to my brother, David, who encouraged me to publish *Rupert's Diary* and introduced me to my editor, Sue Shade. She has helped me every step of the way to take Rupert on a journey from written notes to laptop to publication. I would like to thank her for her thoroughness, expertise, and never-ending support.

Finally as their human, I would like to thank my cats, past and present – George, Tilly, Sam, Rupert, Meg, Rosie and Raffles. You know that you have always made me smile – every single day.

Tuesday 31 July

My human wouldn't get up today.

I put one claw up her snout and still she wouldn't get up. I lined up a great big dribble right by her eye and still she wouldn't get up. I ate the tissue she used to wipe her dribbly eye with and still she wouldn't get up! I went off huffing and puffing to tear at the landing carpet, and then she did get up.

We played the biscuit game, me and my human. I won 2–0! She said I was clever. I know that! She gave me chicken for senior cats. I love chicken for senior cats.

Very hot today in my fur, so I went sleeping in the shade in my back garden. Met Brandy near the sheds. He was snoring and snuffling really loudly – must be because he's such an old boy. I tapped his whiskers and woke him up. He told me to piss off. I told him to piss off back, and then we sat together for a bit until he went off for a piddle!

Had a good day.

AUGUST

My human forgets to go to work!

Wednesday 1 August

My human got up early and gave me rabbit for senior cats. I love rabbit for senior cats.

No time for the biscuit game as she was off out with more humans. They came to see me in the garden, but I hid on my favourite shed. I'm not talking to strange humans. They might put me in a pie.

My human came back very late and gave me chicken and turkey for any old cats. I love chicken and turkey for any old cats. She gave me a cuddle. She smelt of half a lager and told me she'd seen my big cousin, the tiger, on the telly. Has she gone completely mad?

He can't fit on the telly.

Thursday 2 August

My human captured Meg early today and put her in the cat prison box and took her to see Mr Muppet.

Ha ha ha! I know why!

Nasty Cheese smacked her one up the bum and gave her a bottom boil. Meg said that wasn't true and Mr Muppet wanted to see her cos she's so pretty. I told her not to tell such porcupines cos I've seen the human stuffing pink tablets down her. Meg went huffing and puffing down the garden and ate a fly in temper.

My human stayed out all day in the pouring raining time and came home late smelling of two halves of lager. What is the matter with her? She's forgotten to go to work all week!

Friday 3 August

I can't believe it!

My human got up early and put me in the cat prison box and took me to Mr Muppet! I haven't got a bottom boil!

Sat in the waiting room near a smelly dog with a huge snout full of big, big teeth. I puffed myself up and did some serious spitting. My stupid human said "Hello, darling" to stupid snouted dog and tickled it lots.

Mr Muppet didn't dare try to put a glass stick up my bottom, but he put a needle in my fur. I did some really, really serious growling and lots of huffing and puffing. My human and Mr Muppet were well scared!

Soon back home in my garden. Had a good rest of the day sniffing, snoozing, stretching, and piddling. Decided to get my own back on my human by being sick on the bed in the spare room.

P.S. My human gave me tuna fish for senior cats and played the biscuit game. I won 4–0!

Saturday 4 August

My human got up quite early today and gave me chicken for senior cats. I love chicken for senior cats.

I ate Meg's breakfast too. She left it and I found it before my human could hide it. I thought my human might go to work, but she's completely forgotten to go. I don't know why. Her human sister came down and they went out. I sat on my favourite shed with Meg. It was cold and we were glad of our fur. Meg asked if I thought she was pretty today and I said no.

My human came back very late smelling of dogs, rabbits, horses, half a lager, and three glasses of dry white wine. God only knows where she's been. It was disgusting!

I went huffing and puffing out of my house, bashing my cat flap open very loudly, and down the back garden to do my sleeping.

Sunday 5 August

Woke up feeling queasy and felt a furball coming on.

It took four goes, but I finally got rid of it on the hall carpet. My human was still sleeping, but she shouted out that she hoped I wasn't being sick on the spare bed again. Bugger! I forgot to do it there.

The afternoon was sunny and I could hear Silly Billy, and his sister, Jenny, and Mojo yowling at each other in Peggy the great snouted barking mad dog's garden.

I ignored them. I sat on the deckchairs with my human and did some purring. My human kept smiling at me and telling me how lovely I was and that she loved me. I know that. I love me too. I got too hot in my fur, so I went up onto my favourite shed. Brandy was there. He told me to piss off, so I told him to piss off back and then we sat together for a while snoozing and snoring. I had a good day.

P.S. I think Silly Billy and Jenny must have been teaching Mojo how to yowl at the top-of-the-street cats, should they enter our middle-of-the-street territory. She's only little. Silly Billy and his sister like to teach us middle-of-the-street cats. I don't know why. They're younger than me and even younger than Brandy, so Brandy should do the teaching.

P.P.S. Brandy can't be arsed to do anything apart from snoozing and piddling and telling me to piss off.

P.P.P.S. I like Brandy!

Monday 6 August

At last!

My human got up really early today and made some sandwiches. I thought she'd remembered to go to work. How wrong can a cat be? She came home very late again saying she'd been up to London to visit the Queen's palace. I don't know who she's talking about. What Queen? How many kittens has she had?

P.S. I think I'm getting stressed. Nice supper, though. Rice and vegetables for any old cats, and I think I had some any old meat too.

P.P.S. I love any old meat.

Tuesday 7 August

Meg woke me up really early and said I had to tell her she was pretty.

For God's sake! Persian cats are so stupid. She'll never be as big and as gorgeous as me.

I said to her that I'd say she was pretty if she gave me her breakfast before the human hid it from me. She agreed to this! I ate two breakfasts and then said, "You look pretty today, Meg."

Meg went running down the garden shouting, "Rupert says I'm pretty!"

I shouted out, "Pretty ugly!" and she went huffing and puffing out of the garden all day.

Decided not to stress about my human, but she left the house in the evening and didn't come back for her sleeping time.

P.S. Feel completely stressed!

Wednesday 8 August

I can't believe it!

My human forgot to come home all day. The big man from next door came in to give me my breakfast. I know he won't put me in a pie, but the big man's too big. His feet are too big. I thought he might tread on my tail and make me hiss, so I hid in my garden until he went. Then I ate my chicken and turkey for any old cats. I love chicken and turkey for any old cats.

My human didn't come home for sleeping time. Meg cried under human's bed and I went huffing and puffing into the garden.

Where is my human? How many halves of lagers is she drinking?

P.S. How dare she make me so stressed!

Thursday 9 August

My human came home really early.

She cuddled Meg, who was still crying, and told me she'd been to Monet's garden.

She spent two nights in a garden? Who does she think she is?

My human went sleeping on her bed with me and Meg. We did purring and cuddling and she told us she loved us. She tells us that every day. She's such an emotional responsibility.

P.S. Who is Monet? He better not be a cat. He better not come into my garden. I know what I'd say. I'd say, "Piss off, Monet!"

Friday 10 August

Completely fed up.

My human would not get up out of her bed again. Me and Meg made a plan to get her up. We decided to throw up our furballs at the same time. I did mine on the carpet, right next to my human, and Meg did hers on the spare bed. Still she didn't get up.

I decided to do some purring and pawing on her head, but she liked that and did some more sleeping. I tried to bite off her ugly snout, but it stayed put. She'd look better without her snout and with some fur on her face. All humans are ugly and mine's well ugly.

And then she did get up. She did some kissing and cuddling of me until she saw the furballs and then she cleaned them up instead of getting my breakfast. I couldn't bear it! My human told me and Meg off, but she did give me special poultry for senior cats. I love special poultry for senior cats.

Decided to spend the day sulking and sleeping behind the telly.

P.S. My human tried to groomin' my nether regions today. I smacked her one. Nether regions are cats' business!

Saturday 11 August

My human got out of bed without any fuss and gave me rabbit for senior cats. I love rabbit for senior cats.

We played the biscuit game. I won 2–0! My human told me I was a clever boy. I know that.

Went down my garden and spent the morning on my favourite shed. Meg came too. We had a good time purring and sleeping. Meg looked as though she was thinking, so I asked her what was she thinking about and she said, "I don't know." Stupid cat!

Saw a big bird in my garden eating worms. It made my teeth do the chattering so I charged at it, but it flew away. Bloody birds shouldn't have bloody wings. It's not bloody fair!

My human went out and came back smelling of half a lager and a chicken tikka masala. Needless to say, she's forgotten to go to work. My human once told me that if she didn't go to work, we'd have to live in a cardboard box in the middle of the road. I don't want to live in the middle of the road. What is a cat to do?

P.S. Feeling a bit stressed again.

Sunday 12 August

Cheese came in my garden today.

Cheese is such a horrible cat. I don't know why he always likes to give one a swipe and a bottom boil, and his nose is always scratchy and scabby.

Actually, he's well ugly. His dull grey fur sticks out in a damp sort of way, as though he's just fallen in next door's pond. His pointy teeth stick out the side of his mouth and one of his yellow eyes looks bigger than the other and he uses the big one to stare at you before he launches an attack. I don't like him. He doesn't behave how a middle-of-the-street cat should. My human said, "Rupert, nasty Cheese is in your garden!" I totally ignored her and ran upstairs and hid under her bed.

My human went out again and came back smelling of millions of glasses of dry white wine, and two great big dogs called Oscar and Rosie. It was disgusting! I did some serious huffing and puffing, but she didn't care. She said she quite liked dogs and she'd quite like one to live with us. A snouted dog with me? Has she gone completely mad?

Monday 13 August

Cuddled my human lots this morning.

I wasn't sick and I didn't put a claw up her snout and I only tried to bite it twice.

She said she was going to work for a little while, even though it was the middle of the school holidays. She sounded well pissed off. I say, thank God for that!

When she came back, I did lots of cuddling and purring and pawing for her. She told me I was the best boy cat in the world. I know that.

P.S. I think she's forgotten about a snouted dog.

Tuesday 14 August

I was sitting on the bed this morning, with a claw up my human's snout.

She said, "Rupert, if you do not get your claw out of my nose, I'm going to eat you tonight with a creamy tarragon sauce and a hint of garlic. What's more, a gardener's coming today and he'll eat you too."

I can't believe it! Has she been feeding me all these years so that she can eat me with a gardener? I went huffing and puffing down my garden, straight away, and up onto my favourite shed.

Met Brandy there and thought I'd have a relaxing snooze with him, but my human let a big man in the garden.

She shouted, "Don't worry, Rupert, this big man is the gardener and he's come to dig out all that creeping periwinkle in the south border. If you're a very good boy, he won't eat you in a tarragon sauce!"

Then she giggled at the big man gardener and he smiled at her. It looked like the smile of someone who might eat cats.

Me and Brandy scarpered, but we came back later, when the big man gardener had gone, and did our business in the freshly dug earth of the south border. Spent the rest of the day in my secret den worrying about being eaten.

P.S. Will my human wash me down with dry white wine or half a lager?

P.P.S. Eaten by a big man gardener…how disgusting!

P.P.P.S. Who is tarragon?

Wednesday 15 August

I think my human forgot to get up again today, but when she did, she kept huffing and puffing and charging about.

She captured Meg and put her in the cat prison box again and took her to see Mr Muppet. Later, Meg said that Mr Muppet thought she was very pretty. I told her not to tell porcupines and that Mr Muppet was checking on her bottom boil. Meg said that wasn't true and Mr Muppet had said that she was very pretty. I told her that her ears were too furry, and so she smacked me one.

So then I told her that her ears were too furry and her ankles were too thick, and so she smacked me one again.

So then I told her that her ears were too furry, her ankles too thick, and that she had a bottom boil, and then she said, "Mr Muppet says my bottom boil's nearly better." And I said, "GOTCHA!"

Meg smacked me one again and went huffing and puffing down the garden.

P.S. My human came home late smelling of three glasses of dry white wine and roasted pig. That's disgusting, but at least she didn't eat me with the big man gardener. I think she might have been joking because she's always kissing me and telling me how much she loves me.

I did lots of purring and dribbling with her when she came home, just to remind her how much she needs me.

P.P.S. My human has found my secret den. How did she do that? It's a secret.

Thursday 16 August

Woke up early.

Went out into the garden and got the wind up my tail. Felt all catty and scratchy. Came back in and tore up the carpets and smacked Meg.

The wind stayed up my tail all day. I did a lot of running and catching and biting of things. I even ran up a tree, which was a shame cos I got stuck and my human had to get me down. I licked my paws and ran off, hoping that Brandy didn't see. I don't think he did cos when he saw me, all he did was tell me to piss off.

Thank God for that!

Friday 17 August

Meg looked like a compost heap today.

She was full of twigs and leaves and two slugs. I asked her where had she been and she told me she'd been looking for a boyfriend. I told her it was easy to find a boyfriend: all she had to do was put her tail in the air and start yowling. She said, "I did, and Cheese cat smacked me one."

I said, "He's been catstraighted. He can't be arsed with girls."

She said, "I know that. The only thing he gives pretty girl cats is bottom boils." Meg laughed and I laughed. We sat on my favourite shed together and did some sleeping and purring.

P.S. My human ate pig sausage for her tea. I can't believe it! Pig sausage and dry white wine is disgusting.

P.P.S. I really don't think she'll ever eat me, even if I put my claw up her snout every day. She likes pig sausage too much.

Saturday 18 August

My human gave me tuna for senior cats today. I love tuna for senior cats.

She wanted to play the biscuit game. I won as usual, 4–0!

Decided to spend the day on my favourite shed, but had to go back in my house cos Peggy the great snouted barking mad dog went barking mad in her garden. Great noisy snouted animal! And then it started really heavy raining time in the garden. My furry slippered paws got very wet and so did my furry coat. They took a lot of cleaning and groomin' back indoors, but I soon looked gorgeous again. Meg went out in the raining time. She came back soaking and looking like a great-headed rat what with her ugly grey fur. I asked her why had she gone out in the raining time and she said, "I don't know!"

Stupid cat!

Sunday 19 August

My human gave Meg a big groomin' today.

Meg can't look after her fur. She's got too much and her brain is too small to concentrate on her own groomin' for long. Meg lay on her back with her legs in the air and let our human comb her all over, which made her fart and sneeze. Our human got out all the leaves and twigs and the dried-up slugs. Meg looked very pretty and fluffy for one minute. Our human told Meg that she was a very pretty girl. She puffed up very pleased with herself and then she ran out into the garden and into the raining time again. I expect she went off to look for a boyfriend.

My human tried to groomin' me. I don't know why. I'm good at sorting out my own fur and it's always silky and gorgeous. I let her comb my golden furred back, but I didn't let her near my snowy white underbelly and nether regions. She has more sense now than to try. She knows I'll smack her one!

P.S. Meg came back late and soaking wet, full of twigs, leaves, and slugs. If she were my actual litter sister, instead of my younger and irritating housemate sister, she wouldn't be half so dim!

Monday 20 August

Spent the morning in my secret den down the garden.

My human brought a little human to see me in my secret den. I couldn't believe it! How dare she show off my secret den! It's mine! It's a secret!

I went huffing and puffing out of my garden. Met Silly Billy. He said he was fed up with humans and was going off to find a jungle of his own to build his own life. I wouldn't do that. With my fur, I think I'm meant to live in a cold forest. I am a Norwegian Forest cat, but I don't want to live in a cold forest. It would be too cold. And what would I eat? I can't catch birds with their wings on. I can't eat rabbits with their fur on. I'd have to eat worms or become a vegetarian. That's disgusting!

Cuddled my human lots in the evening and she gave me gourmet rice and something for my supper. I love gourmet rice and something. She announced that she wasn't going to work for two whole weeks. She hasn't been for ages. I think she has gone completely mad.

P.S. Tried not to get stressed.

P.P.S. I could be living alone and cold in a very cold forest.

P.P.P.S. I could be living alone and cold in a very cold forest and I could be starving.

P.P.P.P.S. I could be living alone and cold in a very cold forest and I could be starving and I could be eating worms.

P.P.P.P.P.S. Feeling really stressed!

Tuesday 21 August

Thought I'd pretend to live in a cold forest today.

But I was too hot in my fur so I gave up pretending.

Sat with my human on the deckchairs in the garden and she fed me fish biscuits. I love fish biscuits. Then she said that the gardener was coming again today to do some more work and she promised that he wouldn't eat me because he didn't like tarragon.

I couldn't believe it! Why does he have to come in my garden again, and how does she know that he won't eat me without tarragon?

I went huffing and puffing onto my favourite shed and spent the rest of the morning spying on the big man gardener. He mowed and edged the lawn, and made the grass neat around the paving stones. He got very hot and took off his shirt.

My human made him three cups of coffee and did a lot of giggling and smiling. The big man gardener did some smiling back and then he left. Thank God!

I did some sleeping on my favourite shed until Meg woke me up. She asked me if she looked pretty today and I told her no, because her eyes were all bunged up. So she smacked me one.

My human came down the garden and said, "Meg, your eyes are all bunged up. You'll have to go to Mr Muppet." Meg ran away all night!

My human was well cross!

Wednesday 22 August

My human captured Meg very early and took her to Mr Muppet. Meg cried and cried and cried.

Meg came back and said that Mr Muppet said she was very pretty. I smacked her one and human put some cream in her eye. She went huffing and puffing down the garden and sat on my favourite shed with Brandy, but he told her to piss off with her bunged-up eyes. She went crying off out the garden and I sat with Brandy.

We had a good laugh about Meg and I asked him if he would tell me to piss off if I had bunged-up eyes. He said, "Yes." So I said, "Good." We had a good time.

Thursday 23 August

Met Silly Billy today.

He said he was just popping home for his tea. I asked him if he'd found his own jungle and he said, "Only an urban one." I don't know what he's talking about.

Met Brandy on my favourite shed. He doesn't know what Silly Billy's going on about either so we just had a laugh and a piddle and a sleep.

P.S. I like being with Brandy on my favourite shed. We both have silky shiny golden fur. He could be my dad, but he's not quite as handsome as me. I have a snowy white bib and paws, and I'm gorgeously fluffy with a splendid specimen of a tail.

Friday 24 August

My human's still not going to work!

She was up and out early today. It was very hot, so I found the shadiest part of my garden. Brandy was there. He told me he couldn't be arsed to say 'piss off' today and I replied, "Neither can I, Brandy." We did some sleeping and purring together.

My human came home smelling of freshly squeezed lemonade, which made a nice change.

Saturday 25 August

Meg cries every day now when my human puts the cream in her eye.

My human kisses her, which makes her cry all the more. My human told her that her eye was nearly better now and that she was looking very pretty, and so I told her the same. Meg was so pleased that she ran out into the garden and decided to catch a frog to celebrate her prettiness. She fell into next door's pond, which was a shame. She was very messy and not very pretty, but me and my human didn't tell her that. We're fed up with her crying.

Very, very hot in my fur. Wanted to sleep outside in my secret den in the evening, but the humans next door let lots of other humans into their garden.

They were shouting and laughing and drinking lots of halves of lagers. And they were cooking meat. What was it? Pig? Poultry? Or Cat? You can never trust a human. It could be cat! It could be me!

I ran into my house and hid with my human. She shut all the windows and I got very hot in my fur. She got very hot without her fur. We had a terrible night.

Sunday 26 August

I woke my human by putting the whole of her snout into my mouth and biting it.

She wasn't very pleased, but she wouldn't get up. I tore the carpet right by her bed – twice – but she stayed put. I started to eat the long leads coming out of her radio. She said, "Stop it Rupert, you're not a rabbit, you silly boy." How dare she be so rude!

I went huffing and puffing down my garden. The garden was full of strange things such as a can that smelt like half a lager, a big ball, a chocolate biscuit, an animal bone, and a pretend monster head with big teeth. My human came out, eventually, and threw them into next door's garden. I don't know why. It must be a human thing.

Cuddled my human in the evening. I like cuddling my human, even if she is ugly.

Monday 27 August

My human gave me rabbit for senior cats for my breakfast. I love rabbit for senior cats.

I got lots of fish biscuits too.

I hid in the flowers and bushes outside the front door today, and would only come back when my human fed me fish biscuits.

She doesn't like me to escape outside the front. She told me that because we live in a terraced house and I can't get back in by myself, she thinks a human might catnap me and put me in a pie, or a car monster might get me. She does a lot of calling and fretting for me, so I go out on purpose and only come back for my fish biscuits. Meg copies me. I don't know why. She doesn't even like fish biscuits.

Paddy cat was out the front too. He lives on my door mat because he doesn't like his human, or his house, any more. He's convinced his human doesn't feed him enough or love him. He looks all right to me. He's not a posh pedigree, but his grey and white coat is in good condition. My stupid human gave him some fish biscuits too. Damn that cat. They're my biscuits!

My human went out hunting for food for senior cats today. She came back with loads. She's clever like that. She gets a good catch every week.

Then she went out in the evening and came home smelling of bubbly dry white wine and pig sausage. I'm getting fed up with her disgusting ways. I nearly smacked her one, but she said she'd been bitten by a hamster. Serves her right!

P.S. What is a hamster?

P.P.S. What is a terraced house?

Tuesday 28 August

My human got up really early.

She was in a really good mood. She loved playing the biscuit game with me. I won 5–0!

My human was out all day. Pickle came to visit me and Meg. He said, "May I come in your garden, Rupert?"

I said, "OK, Pickle."

He said, "May I come in your house and eat Meg's breakfast biscuits, Rupert?"

I said, "OK, Pickle."

He said to Meg, "Would you care to do some yowling and have Pickle up your bottom, Meg?"

She said, "No thank you, Pickle. I'm sleeping."

He said, "OK, Meg."

Pickle's so polite and well-spoken. He always looks well smart with his white bib and silky black coat groomed to perfection. You'd never believe that horrid Cheese cat is his son. They're like chalk and cheese, Cheese and Pickle. We like Pickle, me and Meg do.

My human came home really late saying she'd been to Bath and the train had broken down.

I was very cross and wasn't going to be her friend, but she gave me two posh suppers and a big cuddle, so I did a bit of purring.

P.S. I thought Bath was upstairs.

Wednesday 29 August

Pissed off and fed up today.

Don't know why. I just felt all catty and scratchy. Went huffing and puffing everywhere.

Met Brandy and yowled, "PISS OFF, BRANDY!" And he told me to PISS OFF, MYSELF! We enjoyed that.

And then, the bloody big man gardener turned up again. I'm getting well fed up with him in my back garden, but my stupid human says she's going to let him out there every week now. How dare she! And she keeps giggling and bringing him cups of coffee. This time, she even baked him a banana cake. He liked that and did a lot of smiling at my stupid human.

Spent the evening in my secret den, ignoring my human. She didn't get a single cuddle out of me.

P.S. Serves her right!

P.P.S. I must admit that the big man gardener edged the lawn to a very good standard today.

Thursday 30 August

Decided to chill out.

I lounged in the flowers in my back garden, but my human was really irritating. She kept chucking all sorts of things out of the two sheds and taking them away in her car monster. She did this all day. She's the one who needs to chill out and do some serious lounging. She's always huffing and puffing for the wrong reasons.

P.S. Nasty Cheese bottom-sprayed all over my flowers, and then did a great big poo in the middle of my lawn. He did it on purpose without any digging. Disgusting animal! My human cleared it up.

P.P.S. I don't know why she's got two sheds.

Friday 31 August

Jumped on my human to wake her up.

She got up without too much fuss. It only took a little bit of dribbling.

Two humans came to see her today. One was a very big man with very big feet. Luckily, I was safe on my favourite shed, but my stupid human brought them down to the sheds! She told them that she was hoping to attract a man with her lovely pair of sheds. I don't know what she's talking about, but I think she's gone completely mad. I like the one with the flat roof – it's my favourite – but what's the point of one with a pointy roof? Me and Brandy don't like sitting on pointy things. She can be very inconsiderate, my human.

Decided to spend the rest of the day in my secret

den. Meg found me and we did some purring together. We talked about our human. Meg said she'd never attract a man because she's too ugly, but if she got rid of her snout and grew some fur, she might attract a ferret. We both laughed.

I said to Meg, "What is a ferret?"

She said, "I don't know!"

SEPTEMBER

My human goes to work,
but big men everywhere!

Saturday 1 September

Played the biscuit game really well today before my breakfast. I won 5–0!

My human tore all the paper off the kitchen walls and said that she needed to get it done before she went back to work. I don't really know what she means, but she must have been in a really bad mood. I only tear paper when I'm furious.

Some humans came to help with the tearing of the paper and then my human shared her tea with them. They had roasted chicken and dry white wine. I don't know who she thinks she is letting any old humans into my house to tear paper off our walls. Shame on her!

I did an awful lot of huffing and puffing and went upstairs to hide in my secret den in the spare room. My human came up and found my secret den. How does she do that? It's secret! I was so cross, I did some more huffing and puffing.

P.S. I love a good bit of huffing and puffing.

Sunday 2 September

I had rabbit for senior cats for my breakfast. I love rabbit for senior cats for my breakfast.

Then I went out my cat flap, into the back garden, and saw a foxy! Meg came too. When she saw the foxy, she went hysterical and shot back into the house. This brought out my human. Foxy smelt her straight away with his long snout. He was off really quickly. I expect she smelt disgusting to foxy.

I stayed on my favourite shed with Brandy. We're not scared of foxy! We just did some sleeping and farting.

Meg calmed down and spent the day in Mojo's garden talking about groomin' and ear fur. They're silly little animals together, Meg and Mojo. They call themselves 'the pedigree princesses' because Meg's a big fat fluffy Persian and Mojo's a little sandy and chocolate-coloured Siamese. They think they're better than me! I am really a Norwegian Forest cat, but once, when I was younger, a nasty vet lady told my human that I was, in fact, a very common domestic moggy with bad manners.

P.S. My human still says I'm a Norwegian Forest cat and Mr Muppet doesn't disagree with her when we visit. My human loves Mr Muppet.

P.P.S. Maybe I'm a common domestic Norwegian Forest cat.

P.P.P.S. I quite like Mojo. She has blue eyes and big ears!

Monday 3 September

Meg woke up my human really early with a frog.

Meg was yowling and meowing and the frog was

leaping all over the bathroom. My human got up and thanked Meg and told her that she was a clever girl. And then my human caught the leaping frog and put it straight back in the garden! She doesn't appreciate presents.

My human looked very miserable today. She said she had to go back to work for a while. When she came home, she had to lie down on the sofa. I did some sleeping with her and she woke me up to tell me that I was snoring. Well, I don't know I'm snoring cos I'm sleeping. I nearly smacked her one, but she got up and gave me posh chicken and turkey for my tea. I love posh chicken and turkey for my tea.

Tuesday 4 September

Was glad of my fur today.

Went out in my garden early, and a cold wind was howling. I think the summertime is going again. My human will be even more miserable. She would be glad of some fur because she's mainly just skin – that's disgusting! My human cheered up, though, when she let big man gardener into my garden again. He kept his shirt on today, but still did digging and mowing. My human did smiling and giggling. She made four cups of coffee and a Victoria Sandwich cake. Big man gardener was well pleased.

Brandy watched them too, on my favourite shed with me, and he said, "You better watch those two, Rupert."

P.S. I am watching them. He knows I'm watching

them. He's been watching me watch them. He's been watching them too!

P.P.S. Still don't know what a ferret is. Must find out.

Wednesday 5 September

My human gave me a pouch of rabbit chunks for any old cats today. I love rabbit chunks for any old cats, but it wasn't enough, so I pinched Meg's breakfast before my human could hide it.

Meg said, "I don't care!"

I said, "Why don't you care?"

She said, "I want to eat carrots."

I said, "CARROTS? Why carrots?"

She said, "I want to be a rabbit with a wobbly nose. They're really pretty and they've always got a boyfriend."

She's such a stupid animal.

So I said, "I eat rabbits without their fur on." Then I said, "And foxes eat rabbits with their fur on."

Meg said, "I don't want the foxy to eat me."

I said, "You'd better stay a cat then."

Meg said, "OK, Rupert." And then she went off to ask Pickle to be her boyfriend for the day.

I did some snoozing in my compost bin, which was full and warm. I felt quite relaxed because my human went to work all day. I think she's going to remember to go every day from now on. Thank God for that! No cardboard box in the middle of the road for me!

P.S. Feeling a little calmer.

Thursday 6 September

My human's definitely going to work.

She got up with the birdies today and she didn't look too happy either! I went off early about my business.

I went to Brandy's garden and found him on his shed. He told me to piss off and I asked him what a ferret was and he said that he didn't know, so I told him to piss off himself. We enjoyed that.

I went back to my favourite shed. I met Silly Billy on the way. I said, "How's your urban jungle, Silly Billy?"

He said, "It's a dismal decaying sprawl used to house the disenfranchised proletariat."

I said, "No wonder you're called Silly Billy, and I bet you don't know what a ferret is."

He said, "A ferret is a half-tamed species of polecat. It is a furry mammal with a long body, a tail, four short legs, and a snout. It has sharp teeth and enjoys darting down the trousers of humans to nibble on their bits and pieces."

I said, "Disgusting animal! Do you think one will go out with my human?"

He said, "It is highly unlikely that the two species would find each other attractive. Coupling and proliferation would be totally out of the question."

I don't know what he's talking about, so I smacked him one and went off for a piddle and a sleep.

P.S. Meg had a great time today. She coughed up a huge furball on the spare bed, caught a frog, ate a moth, and played pretend biting and fighting with me all around the garden. Then we discussed ferrets in the compost bin, which was full of freshly cut grass. I like my sister Meg today, I do!

P.P.S. I don't know what's the matter with Silly Billy's head. He's only six and it's completely full up with dogs' dribble.

Friday 7 September

I can't believe it!

Horrid Cheese cat ambushed me on my favourite shed. I tried to squeeze slowly past him, but my whiskers told me I couldn't get by. He backed me into a corner, staring at me with his wonky eye. He hissed at me without the aitch, so he 'issed at me, and then he leapt on me and rolled me over and over. I rolled right off my favourite shed! I don't want to talk about it.

P.S. He scratched my nose.

P.P.S. My nose really hurts.

P.P.P.S. No sign of a bottom boil.

Saturday 8 September

My human didn't go to work today.

I tried to get her up by heaving up a great big furball on the kitchen mat. She came down to see and then went back to bed. She didn't even clear it up! That's disgusting!

I had to go sleeping on her bed and she kept fretting about my poorly nose. I hate that Cheese cat. He's ruined my gorgeous looks.

P.S. Still no sign of a bottom boil.

Sunday 9 September

I've got a big scab on my nose and it keeps making me go boss-eyed.

I was so cross about it that I put one claw up my human's snout when she was sleeping and then I pulled and pulled. It woke her up and made her eyes water. Now she's got a poorly snout too.

Went in the garden and told Meg what I'd done and she laughed, but Silly Billy was there and he said I was mean and that it was a bit short-sighted to bite the hand that feeds me. He's so stupid! I shouted at him that snout pulling was completely different from hand biting. He tutted and stormed off.

I did feel a bit mean by the evening so I gave my human a big cuddle, even though she was drinking dry white wine and eating soft French cheese. She said she loved me and I was glad about that.

P.S. I've still got my scab.

P.P.S. Still no sign of a bottom boil.

Monday 10 September

My human's definitely going to work.

She got up really early and looked well pissed off. She wouldn't play the biscuit game properly, but she gave me beef for any old cats. I love beef for any old cats.

Spent the day on my favourite shed with Pickle. He said, "May I sit on your shed with you, Rupert?" I said, "Of course you may, Pickle."

We had a nice time. I think Pickle looks up to me. After Brandy, I am the oldest of us middle-of-the-street cats and I'm well handsome and obviously intelligent.

My human came home with lots of books and spent all evening filling them with coloured highlighters and pens. She kept muttering about the "soddin' new feedback policy" and had to have a glass of wine to calm down. I don't know why she's so stressed.

P.S. I've still got my scab.

P.P.S. I don't think I've got a bottom boil.

Tuesday 11 September

Meg was trapped all day.

My human shut her in the wardrobe and went to work! When she got home from work, she kept calling for Meg in the garden and then she eventually found her in the wardrobe. When Meg got out, she did a lot of piddling and eating. Every time I asked her if she'd had a good day, she smacked me one.

P.S. Still got my scab.

P.P.S. Definitely no bottom boil.

P.P.P.S. My human is still marking lots of books with her pens and whingeing about the soddin' feedback policy.

Wednesday 12 September

My human keeps giving me food for any old cats.

Has she forgotten I'm a senior cat? She can be very stupid, but then she is only a human.

Only the lucky few are born to be cats. We are, of course, well clever, except for Silly Billy who's very silly. He sat on my favourite shed today. I asked him what he was thinking about and he said, "The theory of relativity and quadratic equations."

I smacked him one as usual.

Decided to snooze on the sofa for the rest of the morning. I thought I'd get some peace and quiet knowing that my human had gone to work, but all of a sudden the big man gardener let himself into my house through the front door! He unlocked the back door and let himself into my garden! HOW DARE HE! He even said, "Hello Rupert."

I scarpered to my favourite shed.

Brandy was there and we both watched him. He did his usual digging and mowing and edging and even a bit of pruning. He made the garden look well smart. Then he went into the kitchen, made himself a cup of coffee, and came out eating a bit of human's chocolate cake!

Brandy said that I *really* needed to watch him. I told Brandy very loudly that I AM watching him. He knows I'm watching him. He's been watching him with me watching him all morning! How many times do I have to explain this?

P.S. Still got my scab.

P.P.S. My bottom's fine.

P.P.P.S. My human came home and put the colours all over the books again, and then threw one in the air, shouting, "For God's sake!"

Thursday 13 September

My human gave me tuna for senior cats. Thank God for that! I love tuna for senior cats.

My nose felt chilly in the garden today. I think the wintertime is coming on. Even Meg's starting to grow her cold-weather fur. Her ankles look even fatter and her bottom's enormously fluffy.

She said, "Does my bum look big in this fur?"

I said, "Yes."

She went off huffing and puffing into Mojo's garden, but she soon came back cos Mojo's caught fleas! We hate fleas, me and Meg do. Creeping crawling creatures, living off fat cats. They're disgusting!

P.S. Still got my scab, but my bottom's gorgeous.

Friday 14 September

My human gave me posh chicken and turkey for my breakfast. It is for any old cats, but I still love posh chicken and turkey.

Silly Billy spent the whole day jumping over sheds and climbing up trees. He caught a mousie and ate it in my flower bed. He left the tail, so we played flicking it about a bit.

I said to him, "What are equatic equations? Are they biscuits you can eat?"

He shot up and down a tree and shouted, "Quadratic equations, Rupert! Quadratic equations! And no, you don't eat them! You work them out, but you never will because you're cerebrally challenged!"

And then he smacked me one. I couldn't believe it!

P.S. My human picked my scab today.

P.P.S. I have a scar on my nose.

P.P.P.S. My human's sister and her big man came to stay. They're sleeping in my house! How dare they! What's more, big man gardener popped round for a glass of wine with them. Why would he do that?

Saturday 15 September

I can't bear it!

The big man and the sister are still in my house! And then the humans moved the table in the dining room and more big men came and filled it with boxes.

I CAN'T FIND MY BISCUITS AND MY MEAT BOWLS!

I can't find my litter tray and I'm full up with poos!

I'm not talking to my human. Just as well, cos she went out with her sister and the big man, and the big man gardener, and came back smelling of millions of glasses of dry white wine, and the big men smelt of Guinness.

For God's sake!

P.S. Fur growing over my scar.

Sunday 16 September

I can't bear it…again!

The big man and the sister are still here in my house and my dining room's full of big boxes.

My human's other sister came today and they all ate

roasted chicken. I ignored them all day and sat on my favourite shed.

Brandy came to see me. He told me to piss off, and I said, "Piss off yourself, Brandy!"

Then we did a bit of lounging about together and stretching and twisting and yawning. Thank God for a bit of normality.

P.S. More fur growing over my scar.

P.P.S. Big man gardener ate some roasted chicken too. I don't know why he keeps coming round my house.

Monday 17 September

Life is getting unbearably bad.

The big man and the sister are still here.

I can't play the biscuit game cos the dining room's still full of big boxes and THEN, when my human went to work, lots of big men came flying into my house and chucked out the kitchen.

It was full of holes, and then the big men started to take the big boxes from the dining room into the kitchen.

I thought my human would be well mad when she came home, but she didn't seem to care. What's the matter with her?

P.S. Found my litter tray and got out all my poos.

P.P.S. More fur growing back over my scar.

P.P.P.S. Spent the night in the kitchen with Meg. We played jumping in the holes and hiding in boxes. Meg ate a spider.

Tuesday 18 September

My whole life is in chaos!

Big men everywhere! I hid on my favourite shed.

Brandy came to see me and we did some snoozing.

I said, "Well say piss off, for God's sake, Brandy!"

He said, "No."

Dammit!

P.S. My fur's grown back. I look gorgeous.

Wednesday 19 September

The big man and the sister left today, but the other big men are still in my kitchen.

I hid under the bed in the spare room with Meg all afternoon. Pickle crept passed the big men and came to visit. He said, "May I hide under the bed with you, Rupert and Meg?"

We said, "Certainly, Pickle."

We had a nice time snoozing and snoring and farting. Well, Meg did the farting, as usual.

P.S. Big man gardener made the garden look well smart again in the morning. Meg kept wrapping herself around his legs with her tail in the air. She said she liked big man gardener.

P.P.S. I don't think big man gardener likes Meg. He kept sneezing when she was around.

Thursday 20 September

The big men came for a little while and then they left.

I can't believe it! They seem to have left behind a

brand new kitchen! My human spent all night sorting out the dining room and then we all went sleeping happily, but before we did, me and my human played the biscuit game. I won 5–0!

P.S. Beginning to de-stress.

P.P.S. Feeling quite relaxed actually.

P.P.P.S. I'm gorgeous.

Friday 21 September

Got up early and went off to Brandy's shed to tell him about the new kitchen.

Silly Billy was there, so I asked him what he was doing.

He said, "I'm trying to get Brandy to recite poetry."

So I asked him what he was talking about, and Brandy told me to piss off.

I said, "Now I understand. I can recite poetry too. Listen. Piss off, Brandy."

Silly Billy smacked us both one and ran up a fir tree. Me and Brandy are very worried about him. We think he's definitely gone completely mad.

Thank God, I'm an intelligent cat.

Saturday 22 September

My human's got a new cupboard in her new kitchen full of food for senior cats and any old cats.

She's caught loads of the stuff. She gave me rabbit for senior cats. I love rabbit for senior cats.

We played the biscuit game and I won 4–0! Life

seems to be back to normal.

My human then went out all day and came back smelling of roasted bird and two glasses of dry white wine. How normal is that? Totally normal!

Thank God!

P.S. I think I smelt a bit of big man gardener on her.

Sunday 23 September

I can't believe it!

My human let another big man in the house today. He stuck tiles all around the kitchen.

Me and Meg hid under the bed in the spare room.

I said, "If you keep farting, I'll smack you one."

Meg farted, so I smacked her one.

P.S. Spent the evening cuddling my human. I did a lot of dribbling, but she didn't mind.

Monday 24 September

My human raced me down the stairs today.

She says, "Ready! Go!" I don't know why she bothers. I always win our races down the stairs cos she's only got two legs and I've got four!

She then went to work and there was not a single big man in the house! Happy cat Rupert!

P.S. My human said she had a lot of planning and marking to do, and spent the evening playing with her coloured pens. She seemed quite happy and didn't throw a single book in the air. We both had a good day.

Tuesday 25 September

Silly Billy came to see me today.

He said he'd come to apologise to me, and so I asked him what for, and he said for smacking me one.

I told him I was pleased because I'm fed up with him smacking me one, and he said, "I know, being cerebrally challenged and as dim as you is no excuse for smacking you one. I need to exercise more self-control and use my mind to resolve my frustrations when I'm attempting to cope with your utter stupidity."

I said, "Are you calling me stupid?"

He said, "Yes."

So I smacked him one. I had a good day.

P.S. Big man gardener let himself into my garden again today. He left it very neat and the lawn looks very well cared for, but I wish he would bugger off. It's MY GARDEN!

P.P.S. What's more, another big man came into my house and put down a new kitchen floor.

P.P.P.S. What is it with my human and big men?

Wednesday 26 September

My human's gone mad!

I was only scratching up the hall carpet and she shouted, "Stop it, Rupert, or I'll send you off with a flea in your ear."

A flea in my ear? A FLEA IN MY EAR! She knows I hate fleas. How could she put one in my ear? I thought she loved me!

I went huffing and puffing down my garden, so she had to go to work without playing the biscuit game. Serves her right!

My human came home and made roasted pig. She ignored her books and coloured pens and instead changed her clothes, which she never normally does. Then the big man gardener came round and ate the roasted pig with her, and then they drank millions of glasses of dry white wine. Sauvignon blanc, I think. Then she did some cuddling with the big man gardener, and then she did some kissing. How dare she! Kissing and cuddling is what she normally does with me.

I went huffing and puffing down my garden and sat in the compost with Meg, but she decided to go and see the big man gardener. He went home soon after that.

Thursday 27 September

My human gave me rabbit for senior cats today. I love rabbit for senior cats.

Decided to like my human again. She hasn't put a flea in my ear. She gave me a big cuddle before she went to work and told me I was her precious poodle.

I asked Meg what a precious poodle was, but she didn't know. I went over to Brandy's shed and asked him, but he just told me to piss off, so I told him to piss off back. Then I saw Jenny sitting on the rusty old car monster near my favourite shed. She had been over groomin', as usual, and her tortoiseshell coat gleamed in the sun. She's a very neat cat. She'd die if she caught fleas! I said, "Hi Jenny. What's a precious poodle?"

She said, "It's a dog. It can be a big dog with big teeth or it can be a snappy yappy little dog. Its most notable feature is its wool-like fur which is carefully washed and permed and then coloured one of the many colours of the rainbow, but preferably sky-blue pink."

She's as silly as her brother, Silly Billy. I nearly smacked her one, but I fancy her. So I said, "Thank you for telling me that, Jenny, and now I'm off for a piddle."

I went huffing and puffing back up my garden. I can't believe it! My human thinks I'm like a snouted snappy yappy dog with sky-blue pink permed fur. PERMED FUR, for goodness' sake!

P.S. At least no sign of big man gardener today.

Friday 28 September

The summertime came back today.

I was very hot in my fur, and Meg was beside herself with her wintertime bottom and fat ankles. We rested together on our shady shed. I told Meg I fancied Jenny.

Meg said, "She's not as pretty as me. She's not a pedigree, with that common old tortoiseshell coat of hers." And then she smacked me one.

So I said, "And she hasn't got a big bum and fat ankles." Meg smacked me again and went off huffing and puffing, shouting, "Well, you, Rupert, are just a common moggy with ginger splodges on your nose. At least I'm a pretty pedigree Persian princess who comes from Surrey!"

I shouted, "What's Surrey?"

She shouted, "I don't know!"

P.S. How dare Meg say I have ginger splodges on my nose. They're golden!

Saturday 29 September

My human spent all day putting paper back on the kitchen walls. How ridiculous is that?

If she hadn't been in such a bad mood, tearing it off the walls in the summertime, she wouldn't have to spend all day putting it back on now. I don't know who's more stupid, Silly Billy or my human. I smacked them both one today.

My human went out in the evening and came back smelling of millions of glasses of dry white wine and big man gardener. When she shut the front door, she wobbled all over the place. I don't know why. She thought she was quite funny and kept giggling. I kept my distance. Her walk was so wobbly, she nearly stepped on my tail!

Sunday 30 September

My human was as lazy as a lazy cat today.

We laid on the sofa together. She said that the kitchen was utterly and finally finished and she could now have a relaxing day. We had a nice time snoozing and cuddling. She should be a lazy cat more often.

I quite liked my human today. She didn't drink a single glass of dry white wine, but she did get up and eat some roasted pig, which was pretty disgusting. We both ate it.

P.S. I wonder if the kitchen being finished means no more big men in my house. That would make Rupert a very happy cat!

P.P.S. Hope it means no more soddin' big man gardener too. That would make Rupert a very, very happy cat!

OCTOBER

Trauma with Toad, Tail, Wing, and Big Man Gardener!

Monday 1 October

I had a good adventure last night.

I went into my garden and then I climbed up on the sheds and over the walls and down by the big garages and into Scary Alley where the scary things might get you. None of us know what the scary things are exactly, but we've all heard rumours of cat-stealing humans and cat-killing dogs and cat-squashing car monsters and even cat-tearing-to-pieces monsters!

It's the middle-of-the-street cats' boundary and a good meeting place, but if you venture there on your own, you have to keep your paws and whiskers about you!

Jenny and Silly Billy were there. I could hardly tell them apart. They were a mass of mackerel and tortoiseshell, brown and tan fur. I could just see a little bit of Jenny's white bib as they huddled close together, crouched on the ground. Jenny was moving a stone about. I asked them what they were doing and they said that they were playing chess.

I just ignored them and went along the grassy path to the pavement out the front of the houses, and then I couldn't quite remember where to turn around and go back down the grassy path, back to Scary Alley, back by the big garages and over the walls, and onto my sheds again. I had to climb all over the front garden walls until I arrived at my front door, and then I could not get in my house cos my human would not wake up and open the door!

As usual, Paddy cat was sleeping on my door mat, pretending his human doesn't love him. Whenever I see Paddy cat, I smack him one. When he saw me coming over the walls, he ran away in case I did smack him one. Paddy cat's scared of me, which is nice.

When my human eventually woke up, she fretted when she saw me on the door step and she quickly let me in and cuddled me and kissed me and cuddled me. She really can't bear it when I end up on the front door mat, so she cuddled me and kissed me some more. Honestly! Doesn't she know I'm a grown animal? I gave her one of my serious grown-up animal looks, but she still kissed and cuddled me.

P.S. My human says I look like a walrus with my serious grown-up whiskers.

P.P.S. What is a walrus?

Tuesday 2 October

My human hid Meg's breakfast in her bedroom today and I found it and ate it.

Ha ha ha!

Meg was well cross. She said I had to say she was pretty, so I said she was pretty.

She said I had to say pretty Persian, so I said she was

a pretty Persian.

She said I had to say pretty Persian pedigree, so I said she was a pretty Persian pedigree.

She said I had to say pretty Persian pedigree princess, so I said, "Piss off, you big-bottomed fat-ankled pain in the arse." So she smacked me one and I smacked her back.

So she smacked me one again and I smacked her back.

So she leapt on me and we rolled over and over and our fur flew all over the bedroom and Meg did some well cross hissing and spitting and then we went huffing and puffing all the way down the stairs and into the garden.

I went on my favourite shed and Meg said she was going back to Surrey.

I said, "What's Surrey?"

She said, "I don't know!"

She's as mad as a snouted dog.

P.S. My human still doesn't smell of dry white wine.

P.P.S. My human still doesn't even smell of half a lager, but soddin' big man gardener came to do the garden and helped himself to human's coffee cake. Dammit!

Wednesday 3 October

Meg didn't come home for her breakfast.

Meg didn't come home for her tea.

Meg didn't come home for my human to groomin' her.

My human did a lot of fretting and calling after Meg down the garden, but still she didn't come home. I started fretting. How can I pinch her food if she doesn't come home?

My human and me went sleeping on the bed, but we did fretting, not sleeping.

P.S. My human still doesn't smell of dry white wine.

P.P.S. My human still doesn't even smell of half a lager.

P.P.P.S. My human smells of fizzy apple juice and water.

Thursday 4 October

My human went to work fretting about Meg, but she still gave me chicken for senior cats. I love chicken for senior cats.

I wanted to play biting and fighting with Meg, but I think she's gone to Surrey.

Decided to go searching for her as far as the rusty old car monster, but I didn't find her or Surrey. Met Silly Billy. I said, "What's Surrey, Silly Billy?"

He said, "It's a well-to-do county full of well-to-do people who own green wellies, Agas, ISAs, horses, Labradors and, if they're nouveau riche, the occasional Persian cat."

I said, "Meg's gone there."

He said, "Meg couldn't navigate herself out of a paper bag, let alone up the A3M. What's more, if she did get up the A3M, she'd still end up lost in the Devil's Punch Bowl."

I said, "Have you gone completely mad?"

He said, "No," and buggered off before I could smack him one.

Friday 5 October

Meg came home early in the morning when the moon was still shining.

She did yowling and crying, and crying and yowling.

My human cuddled her and kissed her, and kissed her and cuddled her. She fed Meg posh tuna and Meg ate it all up!

I said to Meg, "Have you been to Surrey, Meg?"

She said, "Yes."

I said, "What's Surrey, Meg?"

She said, "It's a garage by Scary Alley that you can get locked in."

I knew Silly Billy talked a load of old dogs' dribble!

Saturday 6 October

I'm not talking to my human today.

She keeps kissing and cuddling Meg just because she went to Surrey.

I went huffing and puffing down my garden to do a bit of bottom-spraying around my flower beds, and found Silly Billy looking at a fat toad.

I asked him what he was doing, and he said he was observing the fat toad for scientific purposes. I said I was going to eat it, and he said, "I advise you not to do that, Rupert. If you were to put it in your mouth, it will release a very nasty secretion from its skin that's so bitter you will be dribbling and frothing at the mouth for a very long time." I told him he was speaking dogs' dribble and froth, so I bit the toad and picked the whole of it up in my mouth. That showed him and the toad!

P.S. Spent the evening dribbling and frothing.

P.P.S. My human spent the whole night kissing and cuddling soddin' big man gardener. Dammit! Meg tried to kiss and cuddle big man gardener too. Typical!

Sunday 7 October

Hid under human's bed today and did a bit of snoozing and stretching.

It was scary outside. There was big raining time and the wind was in a terrible mood, yowling and howling and bashing the trees.

My human came home and kissed me, and put me up on the kitchen surface so that I could watch her get my beef for any old cats supper.

She put a fire on under her potatoes, and then all of a sudden she picked me up and threw me in the washing up bowl while screeching loudly in my ears! I got very wet. I was very anxious, what with the screeching and the wetness. I was hysterical!

Meg laughed and said my tail fur had caught on fire. That is such a porcupine!

P.S. I think there's something seriously wrong with my human.

P.P.S. House smelt of singed tail fur all night. It was disgusting.

Monday 8 October

Stupid Paddy cat was staring in through the front door today, begging for food.

My stupid human fussed him and fed him some fish meat for any old cats. I could have eaten that fish meat for any old cats!

I went huffing and puffing down my garden and got my slippered paws wet on the wet, wet grass.

Met little Mojo. She was crying because Cheese had smacked her one and given her a bottom boil.

I like little Mojo, so I told her that with her blue eyes and big ears she was pretty, even with a bottom boil.

She asked me if I really thought she had big ears and I said, "Yes."

She then went off crying into Peggy the great snouted barking mad dog's garden.

I thought I'd cheered her up, but Jenny came and pounced on my tail, and smacked me one for upsetting Mojo by telling her she had big ears.

I'm not talking to girl cats anymore; especially the pedigree ones. They can be very catty, accidentally and on purpose. I'm just going to ignore them!

P.S. My tail fur looks a little singed.

P.P.S. What's wrong with having big ears? All the better for swivelling and hearing.

Tuesday 9 October

Meg wanted to talk to me, but I ignored her.

She asked me why I was ignoring her, and I said that

it was because she was a girl cat, and then she said that I wasn't ignoring her cos I'd just spoken to her, and then I explained that I only spoke to her to tell her that I was ignoring her. We both got confused. Then Meg said that she'd give me her breakfast if I stopped ignoring her. I said, "OK, Meg," and ate her breakfast. I like my sister Meg today.

We played biting and fighting together and flicking worms in the garden. We both got our slippered paws soaking wet, but we didn't care!

P.S. Some of my tail fur seems to have fallen off.

Wednesday 10 October

My human threw all her clothes out of the wardrobe today and said she didn't have a poxy thing to wear to poxy work.

I ignored her. She needs to calm down, grow a fur coat, and drink some dry white wine.

I went huffing and puffing down my garden and left her to it. Met Silly Billy and told him that I hated Cheese cat cos he'd even given little Mojo a bottom boil.

Silly Billy said that he gives everyone a bottom boil, even Silly Billy!

I said that we should all gang up on him and smack him one right out of the neighbourhood, but Silly Billy said that that would never happen. I asked why, and he said, "For one, it is against the laws of cat nature to work together as a co-operative unit for the sake of the common good, and secondly, we live in a dog-eat-dog world."

My God! I can't believe it! I didn't know dogs ate each other – that's disgusting!

P.S. Silly Billy sat with me on my favourite shed and watched big man gardener do the garden. Silly Billy was well impressed with his digging and mowing and edging. I told him about the kissing and cuddling with my human. He said that I'd better watch them. I AM watching them. How could I tell him about them if I wasn't watching them?

Stupid cat! I nearly smacked him one.

Thursday 11 October

Won the biscuit game, 6–0, and beat my human at stair racing! Then I had beef for any old cats. I love beef for any old cats.

Ate Meg's meat too. She said that I was a fat cat and I was well chuffed and told her that I was indeed fat and gorgeous.

Went off for a piddle and a long lovely sleep.

Happy cat Rupert!

Friday 12 October

I just did some more sleeping today. I couldn't be arsed with cat business.

P.S. My human went out and came back really late smelling of chicken tikka masala. I was quite pleased with her, but there's still no sign of dry white wine or half a lager! On the other paw, she did smell of big man gardener.

Saturday 13 October

My human's gone mad again!

She cut down all the plants in the front garden. I can't hide from her now and she won't tease me out with biscuits. Bugger!

I watched from the front door as she made friends with a big man who had a great big huge snouted dog called Floyd. He was as big as a monster and I just stared at him.

He barked, "What are you looking at, you short-arsed, flat-snouted, brain-dead mummy's boy?"

I went huffing and puffing down my garden and nearly wet myself.

P.S. Meg did wet herself.

Sunday 14 October

The wintertime's definitely coming, cos Meg's huge in all her fur now. She looks like a compost heap.

My human did groomin' so many bits of garden out of her today, plant and animal life.

My human also went out hunting again today. As usual, she came back with loads of meat and biscuits for senior cats and any old cats. She put it all in my cat cupboard, and it was good to see. She then spent the afternoon cuddling me. She told me I was the best boy cat in the world. I did some deep purring and a little bit of dribbling.

She loved it!

Monday 15 October

My human gave me tuna for senior cats today. I love tuna for senior cats.

Then she gave some to Paddy cat out the front. Bloody animal! I'm going to smack him one soon.

Spent the day on my favourite shed with Meg. We decided to be on foxy alert. We didn't see him. We haven't seen him for ages. I said to Meg that he was lying low so that he could spring a surprise attack. She asked me what I meant by that, so I told her that he was going to eat her up any day now, but that it would be a surprise. Meg started to cry and then crawled low-bellied, with her ears tucked right back, all the way up the garden and into the house.

Ha ha ha!

P.S. My human spent all night with her coloured pens and books. She looked well pissed off.

Tuesday 16 October

Slept nearly all day and ignored big man gardener in my garden.

Decided to spend the night round the front so I could smack Paddy cat one. I went down by Scary Alley. Silly Billy and Jenny were there, as usual. They were looking at the ground and playing with bits of cheese. I asked them what they were doing and they said that they were playing a game called Trivial Pursuits. For God's sake!

Found my way round the front, but I'd forgotten that

the human had cut down all the plants. I was stuck there – overexposed! I couldn't get back! I couldn't hide in the flowers! Anything could have eaten me! My human didn't open the door until morning time!

P.S. No sign of Paddy.

P.P.S. I wanted to do some yowling and hissing and smacking of him. Dammit!

Wednesday 17 October

Spent the whole day snoozing and de-stressing in my house.

I was looking forward to a relaxing evening, but my stupid human invited big man gardener around. He stayed all evening and did cuddling and kissing nearly all the time.

Meg kept wrapping herself around his legs and this made our human laugh.

Then Meg jumped up on big man gardener and tried to do kissing and cuddling with him too. He did some smiling, and lots of sneezing. I don't think he liked Meg much because he soon started crying and then he cleared off. Good!

P.S. I did a little bit of bottom-spraying on his coat, which he left in the hall. Ha ha ha!

Thursday 18 October

The leaves keep falling off the trees and I can see all the birdies in them.

I watch them swoop into my garden to eat the pears

that have fallen off next door's tree. My teeth start chattering and I make funny noises, so I charge at the birdies and they bloody well fly away! I'm fed up being a cat today. Smacked Meg up the bottom and went sleeping on my sofa.

P.S. My human did her colouring of the books very quickly in the evening. Her markings are becoming very shoddy. She normally takes far more care and time. Then she went out and came back smelling of lots of halves of lager and big man gardener.

Friday 19 October

Spent the whole day charging at birds.

Silly Billy watched me. He said, "Rupert, what are you doing?"

I said, "I'm charging at birds."

He said, "Rupert, cats don't charge at birds."

I said, "What do they do then?"

He said, "Rupert, cats stalk birds in a clever, cunning, underhand manner, and then they pounce unsuspectingly upon their prey."

I said, "That sounds clever, Silly Billy."

He said, "Rupert, it's not clever. It's basic cat instinct; an instinct which you in your pet-eating-food-for-senior-cats-while-your-pathetic-human-smothers-you-in-kisses lifestyle have forgotten! You big fat good-for-nothing creature!"

I said, "Are you calling me fat?"

He said, "Yes."

I said, "Good!"

Saturday 20 October

Ate game and turkey for any old cats, which was quite nice, and won the biscuit game 4–0!

Then I spent the whole day practising my stalking skills with Silly Billy. I caught a stone, a twig, five leaves, and a snail! I was well chuffed. I felt like a wild thing!

Went home exhausted and ate chicken for senior cats, followed by Meg's tea, followed by posh turkey and rice for supper.

Today would have been well good, except big man gardener came around again in the evening and stayed very late.

My human shut the living room door so that Meg couldn't do kissing and cuddling with them. I taught Meg how to bottom–spray, like a boy cat, on his coat before we both went upstairs and sulked under the bed in our secret den in the spare room.

When our human finally came out of the living room, her clothes were very untidy and her hair was all over the place. She looked such a mess, but she seemed very happy.

Then big man gardener left and tripped over Paddy cat on the front doorstep.

Ha ha ha! Again!

Sunday 21 October

Loads of humans came to my house today, including the big man gardener, so I stayed out in my garden.

There were birdies everywhere, so I decided to catch one and eat it. I stalked for hours and hours, and then I POUNCED! And then the bloody thing FLEW AWAY! I can't stand it! Who gave the birdies their wings?

Went on my favourite shed and met Brandy. Told him to piss off and he told me to piss off back.

He has no idea just how pissed off I am!

Monday 22 October

Went out early to find Silly Billy.

I told him that the birds should not be allowed to have wings, and he agreed. He said he might complain to the bird maker and then I'd feel better.

I said, "OK, Silly Billy," and walked away. I have no idea what he's talking about, but I guess he can't help being so stupid!

P.S. Meg was showing off in front of Brandy, practising her balances on the sides of the compost bin. She fell in and jumped out with six woodlice, one carrot, a slice of leek, and a dahlia stuck in her fur. She licked her paws, pretended it hadn't happened, ambled down the garden, and then caught a bird. How does she DO THAT?

Tuesday 23 October

Spent the morning spying on big man gardener from my favourite shed.

He let himself into my garden again and made the garden look very neat and tidy. He even did some digging and swept up the leaves that had fallen off the trees. He went back in the house and came out with a huge piece of my human's cake. Again!

Silly Billy came to join me on my favourite shed and told me what he might say to the bird maker today.

He said, "Mr Bird Maker, I would like to talk to you about the birds and their wing situation…Although some creatures, particularly birds, may argue that it is all right for birds to have wings, I would like to argue that it is not. My first reason for thinking this is that they've got legs, so why do they need wings as well? My second reason is that if they built their nests on the ground, they wouldn't need their wings to fly up to the trees. Furthermore, without wings, us cats could catch them more easily and then Rupert wouldn't be so grumpy. When Rupert is grumpy, he smacks you one. That, frankly, is not nice.

"Therefore, although some birds may argue that they like flying and they don't like being eaten by cats, I think I have shown that in all fairness to Rupert, who is a rubbish hunter, birds should not have wings. Finally, vertebrates don't have them – apart from strange creatures like bats – so why the bloody hell should birds? With kind regards, and in the hope that you are listening and will take my well–argued, persuasive points seriously, from Silly Billy and Rupert…And just to add to my points, they could always use Heathrow in an emergency."

I was dead impressed, so I went home for a sleep.

P.S. What are vertebrates?

Wednesday 24 October

Fed up with my human.

She's too grumpy to play the biscuit game and she's making no effort whatsoever to come home smelling of dry white wine, let alone chicken tikka masala or even half a lager. I left her to it this morning and went huffing and puffing down my garden.

Met Silly Billy by the rusty old car monster.

I said, "Have you spoken to the bird maker yet, Silly Billy?"

He said, "No."

I said, "Why?"

He said, "I don't know who the bird maker is."

I said, "What do you mean?"

He said, "This needs some serious thought, Rupert. I have come to believe that the bird maker must be God. This, therefore, becomes a theological, theosophical, indeed philosophical question. Who, we must ask, is God? Is he an old cat with a beard that lives up in the sky? Is he a fictitious straw to clutch at in times of trouble? Or could he be a mystical being who transcends the universe and, through his omnipresence, works in wondrous ways? On the other paw, have birds just mindlessly, without any purpose or design, evolved from a thundering great dinosaur?"

I said, "Silly Billy, do you know who to speak to or not?"

He said, "Not."

So I smacked him one. I knew I would, and he knew I would, and that's an end to the matter.

P.S. Birds still have their wings and I will never catch one, not by charging or stalking.

P.P.S. I don't want to catch one.

P.P.P.S. Meg says they're all covered in sticky feathers and when you bite them raw their insides come out. That's disgusting! Meg gives hers to our human and she never looks best pleased either.

Thursday 25 October

Decided to have a normal day.

Said piss off to Brandy and good day to Pickle and did a lot of snoozing and a bit of stretching.

P.S. My human went out in the evening and came back smelling of roasted pig and dry white wine! I was so pleased with her. I gave her a cuddle and did some deep purring. She loves to hear my deep purring. Then I smelt a bit of big man gardener on her. Damn him!

Friday 26 October

My human took Meg to see Mr Muppet today.

I said, "Have you got a bottom boil, Meg?"

She said, "No. Mr Muppet just wanted to tell me I was pretty. He looked in my ears, my eyes, my mouth, and up my bottom and then he said I was a pretty girl, Meg."

I said, "As if!"

Then our stupid human said, "Mr Muppet says you're a lovely little girl, Meg. A very pretty little girl, Meg."

Bugger!

Saturday 27 October

My human's gone mad, yet again!

She got up early and gave our sofas away to strange humans at the door.

Later, she let some big men into our house with new sofas. She put our cat blankets on them, but I still don't like the sofas. They don't smell one bit of cats' piddle, furball, or sick! What has she done? It'll take ages to get all my sniffs back!

Spent the day huffing and puffing in my garden and bottom-spraying the plants.

P.S. I'll soon be bottom-spraying the new sofas!

Sunday 28 October

Still not talking to my human.

Meg is. Meg likes the sofas. She says they're just right for a Surrey cat. Silly little animal.

My human invited the big man gardener around in the evening. He sat with my human and Meg on the new sofas. I don't think he liked them very much because he kept sneezing and rubbing his eyes.

Meg came outside to find me in the garden. She told me all about our human and big man gardener sitting on the sofas together. Then she said, "Rupert, I think the big man gardener is going out with our human."

I said, "What do you mean?"

She said, "Big man gardener is our human's boyfriend."

I said, "But he's not a ferret!"

She said, "She's too ugly to attract a ferret, but big man gardener is a very ugly human too, so they make a good match."

I said, "Boyfriend! That's disgusting!"

Monday 29 October

My human has forgotten to go back to work today and she doesn't seem to care.

She spent the day painting things, and lounging on her new sofas. I decided to have one cuddle with her. The sofas are very soft. They're good to lie on. I quite like them. They just need to smell a bit more catty. I'll soon see to that.

P.S. No sign of big man gardener today. Good!

Tuesday 30 October

My human opened the front door today and went outside to talk with the lady next door.

I came out to see what was going on and the humans were both looking at Paddy cat. He was wolfing down a whole bowl of food that the lady next door had put out for him. Chicken for any old cats. I love chicken for any old cats and I live here, not Paddy cat, so I wasn't having that!

I leapt over the little garden wall, jumped on Paddy cat's back and with my front legs and paws around him, I hauled him out of the way and started to wolf down the food myself.

Paddy cat stared at me. My human stared at me.

Then she picked me up and said to the lady next door that she was sorry and that I was a very naughty, greedy boy. The lady next door laughed and encouraged Paddy cat to carry on eating the bowl of food. I did some serious growling, so my human shoved me into my house and told me I was indeed a very naughty, greedy boy. How dare she! Bloody Paddy cat!

P.S. I did not have a good day.

Wednesday 31 October

My human seems to have forgotten that she thinks I'm a very naughty, greedy boy.

She fed me tuna for senior cats for my breakfast. I love tuna for senior cats. Then she played the biscuit game and I won 7–0!

I stayed in with her all day, doing cuddling and dribbling and snoozing. I thought we were having a normal time together, but then she said, "Rupert, if you go out tonight with the witches, don't go flying sky high and tumbling through the Milky Way unless you're wearing your safety harness on the broomstick."

Is she normal? I don't think so.

Is she completely mad? I think so!

Went huffing and puffing down my garden. Met Meg by the light of the full moon. She was out of breath and wide-eyed and I asked her what was up. She said that Mojo said that Brandy said that Paddy said that Pickle said that Cheese had just seen a hobgoblin in Scary Alley.

We were well hysterical and ran indoors to hide

under our human's bed together.

P.S. I can't believe my human would think I'd go out flying high in the sky without my safety harness!

P.P.S. What is a hobgoblin?

NOVEMBER

Something lurks in Scary Alley!
What's human doing with big man gardener?

Thursday 1 November

Slept most of the day.

Too tired to do anything else after the stresses of yesterday.

I know big man gardener spent the morning in my garden because I could hear him mowing the lawn. I was too tired to spy on him, but I bet my human made him six cups of coffee and fed him some of her Millionaire's Shortbread.

In the evening, I met with Meg, Mojo, Brandy, Paddy, and Pickle by the big garages to discuss the hobgoblin. Brandy said that Cheese hadn't actually seen the hobgoblin, but had heard a terrible loud, low growl that was so terrifyingly terrible that it must have been a hobgoblin.

We all shuddered and went home.

Friday 2 November

Saw Cheese today.

I asked him about the hobgoblin, which was well brave of me. He didn't answer. He just growled and smacked me one.

P.S. I hope I don't get a bottom boil.

P.P.S. Cheese's fur was all puffed up, making him look twice as big as he really is, and his tail looked like a pointy bottle brush.

P.P.P.S. He looked as menacing as the most menacing thing ever!

Saturday 3 November

Cuddled my human this morning.

I bit her snout but she didn't mind. She got up and gave me rabbit for senior cats. I love rabbit for senior cats!

Then she gave some rabbit for senior cats to Paddy cat outside the front door. He loves rabbit for senior cats too, but it's my rabbit for senior cats!

Went huffing and puffing down my garden.

Decided to stay out all day and all night to worry my human. Soon came home. The sky was full of lights and fires and big bangs. All the cats ran to their homes, even Cheese. I charged through my cat flap and up the stairs and met Meg under the bed in the spare room.

She said, "Shall we play chess like Jenny and Silly Billy?"

I asked her how we play chess, and she said, "I don't know."

I nearly smacked her one, but instead I said, "Let's play *I spy*."

She said, "OK, let's."

But, we didn't. We couldn't *I spy* anything under the bed, so she did some farting and I did some snoozing.

Then we realised that our human and big man

gardener were together in her bedroom with the door shut. They must have liked the fires, lights, and big bangs because we could hear a lot of squeaking and screeching and a little yowling coming from the room.

Then Meg said that if they were boyfriend and girlfriend, they might be doing some bottom fiddling and yowling, just like cats do.

Meg thought about it and said, "That's disgusting!"

I said, "That's beyond disgusting!"

Sunday 4 November

Big man gardener had gone before breakfast time.

I tried not to think about yowling and bottom fiddling and did some serious kissing and cuddling with my human. She's MY human! I am her special boy and she's always telling me that she loves me. We had a nice time, my human and me, and we even played the biscuit game. I won 6–0! In the evening, we did some more kissing and cuddling, and she ate some chicken and drank two glasses of red wine. By the smell of it, it was quite good quality.

P.S. I slept right next to my human on the bed and did even more kissing and cuddling with her. I stayed there all night and she said that she loved me and that I was her best boy. So there. Ha ha ha, big man gardener!

Monday 5 November

My human went off to work, sulking as usual.

I had a nice, quiet, relaxing day.

My human came home and roasted some pig. We had a good time eating it, even though the big bangs and coloured lights were falling all around our house and garden – for goodness' sake! Me and Meg were well brave. We stayed with our human and didn't go under the bed in the spare room. It's dead boring under the bed. No wonder Meg farts.

P.S. My human threw two books in the air in the evening and did not seem to enjoy using her coloured pens. There were lots of "for God's sake!".

Tuesday 6 November

The weather's getting colder.

I was glad of my fur in the house today. Meg went out in all her fur and came back saying she'd kissed Pickle. I asked her if Pickle liked being kissed and she said that he didn't and that he cried, so I said, "Why did you kiss him then?"

She said, "I don't know."

For God's sake! I hope she never kisses me. I'm a grown animal. I don't want to cry!

P.S. My human smelt of sparkling white wine and pickled onions tonight.

P.P.S. She kissed me.

P.P.P.S. It was disgusting.

Wednesday 7 November

Turned really cold today.

Did some spying on big man gardener in the garden,

but he didn't stay long. He didn't seem too bothered with his mowing and edging and digging today. He spent most of his time in the kitchen, helping himself to coffee and cake.

I decided to stay in too and did some snoozing on the sofas. I quite like them now, even if they are for Surrey cats.

Pickle popped in and asked if he could eat Meg's biscuits. I said that he could, so he did. Then he asked if he could snooze on the sofas for Surrey cats and I said that he could. We had a nice day once big man gardener cleared off.

Pickle scarpered when my human came home. He doesn't like her. She's too soppy for him. I told him how she picks up cats and kisses them: not once, twice, but a million times. He nearly had a heart attack, and flew out the cat flap muttering, "Disgusting human."

My human picked me up and kissed me: not once, twice, but a million times. I didn't mind.

Thursday 8 November

Still really cold, so I stayed in again.

Meg went out in all her fur. I said that her bum was so big, she could sit on an icicle and not know it.

She asked me what an icicle was and I said that it was a big pointy thing.

She said, "That's disgusting," and went huffing and puffing down the garden.

Went for a stroll down my garden later. Saw a dead frog and then sat on my favourite shed for a while.

Met Brandy and told him to piss off. He told me to piss off back, and I said, "I think I will. My ears are too cold out here and my slippered paws are freezing."

He said, "Me too."

So we both pissed off.

Thought I'd do some really big cuddling with my human on the bed to keep us both warm. Jumped up and landed on big man gardener! I was so cross. I bit his nose and snuggled right up close to my human so that they couldn't do any bottom fiddling. My human laughed and cuddled me. I stayed there between them all night. Big man gardener did lots of snuffling and sneezing.

P.S. Meg came home and accidentally coughed up a furball in his shoe. She said it was just the right size for a furball, and then she slept on big man gardener's head.

Friday 9 November

Big man gardener left early again today after our human got up and sorted out Meg's furball in his shoe.

My human then played the biscuit game properly, even though she had to go to work. I won 5–0!

Had mashed up fish for any old cats for breakfast. I love mashed up fish for any old cats.

Ate some of Meg's ham and turkey too, but my human saw and took it off me. Bugger! I nearly hissed at her.

It was freezing again, so even Meg stayed in. We did snoozing all day and we didn't talk once cos I was on the sofa and she was under the bed in her secret den.

When she eventually came downstairs, I asked her where she had been.

She said, "In my secret den."

I said, "Where is your secret den?"

She said, "Under the bed in the spare room."

Saturday 10 November

Spent some time on my favourite shed today.

Met Brandy there and told him about my human and the big man gardener doing bottom fiddling.

He said that big man gardener might move in, and then my human wouldn't love me so much. Then he said they might have a human baby, what with all the bottom fiddling, and then my human would completely forget all about me. He said she would probably forget to feed me because she would spend all her time fussing over the human baby. He said, "Believe me. I know." He sounded quite bitter and not like himself at all.

I was beginning to feel quite hysterical until Silly Billy came by and told me that it was highly unlikely that my human would have a baby. He said that by looking at her, she was quite old. Menopausal or even post-menopausal.

I said, "What does that mean?"

He licked his paws, swished his tail, and said, "Well it means, well…"

Then he just told me not to worry about a baby and cleared off, muttering that human physiology made him sick.

My human went out all day today. I don't think she

was with big man gardener. She came home really late smelling of dry white wine and shepherd's pie.

P.S. I bet that shepherd was well pissed off.

P.P.S. Not as pissed off as I am thinking about that bloody big man gardener!

Sunday 11 November

My human stayed in all day and looked after us cats.

She did groomin' Meg and made her twice as fluffy.

Meg went huffing and puffing down the garden shouting, "My bum's extra big in this now. I'll never get a boyfriend today."

I popped out for a bit and met Jenny by the rusty old car monster. She looked well cross and told me she had heard about my human and that she was disgusted with her.

She said, "I thought your human was an upstanding member of the community. She has let herself down very badly and Jane Austen would be appalled at her improper, alley-cat behaviour."

She jumped down from the rusty old car monster and then turned round and shouted, "What's more, I send no compliments to your human. She deserves no such attention. I am seriously displeased." Then she flounced off!

I don't know what she's talking about, so I went home and watched my human cook some roasted pig. She likes eating animals.

P.S. What if one day she really does decide to eat me with big man gardener?

P.P.S. I'm feeling hysterical.

P.P.P.S. Calmed down a bit. My human kissed and cuddled me and I dribbled and purred for her. I don't think she could do without me.

Monday 12 November

Not so cold today.

Went out in my garden and the dead frog is still there. I flicked it about a bit and then went on my favourite shed. Meg leapt up on it looking wide-eyed and breathless.

I said, "My God, Meg, what's up? Don't tell me that the hobgoblin's still down Scary Alley!"

She said, "I don't know!"

I said, "Well, my God, Meg, don't tell me you've seen the foxy!"

She said, "I don't know."

I said, "Well then, Meg, what do you know?"

She said, "Jenny says that Mojo is going out with Pickle!"

I smacked her one and she went crying into the house to hide in her secret den under the bed.

P.S. Bit worried about the hobgoblin. What if it is still in Scary Alley?

P.P.S. Still don't know what a hobgoblin is.

Tuesday 13 November

Had chicken for senior cats for my breakfast. I love chicken for senior cats.

Hunted down Meg's breakfast. It was under the bed in her secret den. She had eaten all her breakfast. Bugger! She never eats all her breakfast. Maybe she's got worms. I found her on the sofas for Surrey cats.

I said, "Meg, have you got worms?"

She said, "I don't know."

I said, "Have you got wiggly things in your business?"

She said, "What business?"

I said, "Your cat business."

She said, "That's my business!" And then she went out huffing and puffing down the garden.

I did some serious snoozing until Meg exploded through the cat flap all wide-eyed and breathless.

I said, "My God, Meg, you have seen the hobgoblin!"

She said, "I've asked Silly Billy to be my boyfriend!"

I said, "What did he say?"

She said, "I don't know."

What a surprise!

P.S. I wonder if Silly Billy said yes.

P.P.S. What am I going to do about the hobgoblin in Scary Alley?

Wednesday 14 November

Set off early down my garden to find Silly Billy.

He was snoozing in Mojo's garden. I woke him up and said, "Silly Billy, did Meg ask you to be her boyfriend?"

He said, "Yes."

I said, "What did you say?"

He said, "Well, Rupert, although your sister is a fine-looking Persian pedigree from Surrey, with a hint of Burmese about her nose, I had to decline her offer."

I said, "What does that mean?"

He said, "I gently explained to Meg that although she was a beautiful, lovely, fluffy chocolate-box specimen of a cat, I could not cope conversing with such an air-headed, brain-dead neurotic female. Furthermore, since I've been catstraighted and she hadn't felt the urge to wail like a banshee since Pickle went up her bottom many moons ago, there didn't seem much point in stepping out together, because procreation would obviously be fruitless."

I said, "What does that mean?"

He said, "NO, I DO NOT WANT TO GO OUT WITH MEG!"

Broke the news to Meg. She started to cry so I told her that Silly Billy thought she was very pretty and he liked her big bottom. Meg was delighted. She ran down the garden shouting, "Silly Billy thinks I'm pretty! Silly Billy likes my big bottom!"

Stupid cat!

P.S. My human came home really early with the big man gardener. Perhaps she's scared of the hobgoblin too.

P.P.S. Maybe I could get Cheese to check out the hobgoblin.

P.P.P.S. What if Cheese and the hobgoblin got me?

P.P.P.P.S. Feeling really scared.

Thursday 15 November

Really dead brave today.

Went in search of Cheese. Nobody goes looking for Cheese. I found him by the big garages. He'd just eaten a mousie and was licking his lips and purring. I came straight out with it and asked him if he would please go down Scary Alley and scare off the hobgoblin. He said nothing back to me. He just flattened his ears, growled menacingly, and chased me all the way home trying to smack me one as we ran. Thank God he kept missing, because I'm not in the mood for a bottom boil.

Hid under the bed in the spare room feeling hysterical. I think Cheese may be scarier than the hobgoblin.

P.S. What is a hobgoblin? I've never actually seen one, but whenever anyone mentions a hobgoblin, it makes my fur stand on end.

P.P.S. So does Cheese.

Friday 16 November

Decided to spend the day in the spare room under the bed, just in case Cheese or the hobgoblin came looking for me.

My snoozing was interrupted by Meg, who decided to visit her secret den with Pickle. I asked them what they thought they were doing disturbing me under the bed. Meg explained that Pickle was her boyfriend. I asked Pickle what had happened to Mojo. He explained that he only went out with her for an hour last Monday.

Meg said, yet again, that Pickle was her boyfriend and Pickle said that this was true because he'd decided to go out with her for the day. I said, "Why?" He didn't know why. Typical!

We talked about the hobgoblin. We've decided it's a great big huge scary monster with big, big teeth and ugly skin. AND, there's definitely one lurking in Scary Alley.

Meg and I spent all evening cuddling our human. Meg and I spent all night sleeping in our human's bed. The big man gardener didn't like that one bit. He did a lot of sneezing and not one little bit of bottom fiddling.

Ha ha ha!

P.S. Maybe Silly Billy can sort out the hobgoblin.

Saturday 17 November

Too anxious to play the biscuit game today, but I still ate up all my rabbit for senior cats. I love rabbit for senior cats.

Meg and I went off to find Silly Billy. We found him by the rusty old car monster. He was humming with his eyes closed.

I asked him what he was doing and he said that he was meditating.

I nearly smacked him one, but instead I said, "Silly Billy, will you stop meditating and go down Scary Alley and see off the hobgoblin?"

He asked me what I thought a hobgoblin was, so I told him it was a great big huge scary monster with big, big teeth and ugly skin.

Meg added, "And it hisses at you before it eats you."

And I said, "And it eats you very slowly for several days."

And Meg said, "And..."

And Silly Billy said, "Shut up!" So we did.

Then Silly Billy asked who had actually seen the hobgoblin so I told him that Meg had.

Silly Billy said, "When did you see the hobgoblin, Meg?"

She said, "I don't know."

So I said to Meg, "The hobgoblin makes you wide-eyed and breathless," and then I said, "My God, Meg, have you seen the hobgoblin?"

Meg said, "But I haven't seen a hobgoblin."

So Silly Billy asked her what had made her wide-eyed and breathless, and she said that it was when Pickle went out with Mojo.

Silly Billy smacked our heads together and shouted, "There is no hobgoblin. It's just a figment of your strange and hugely limited imagination!"

We said, "What does that mean?"

Silly Billy shouted, "There is no scientific evidence for the existence of a hobgoblin."

We said, "What does that mean?"

Silly Billy smacked our heads together again and screeched, "THE HOBGOBLIN LEFT SCARY ALLEY LAST TUESDAY AND IS NEVER COMING BACK!"

Thank God for that!

He then went off muttering something about how he bet Henrietta, with her very low Abyssinian growl, accidentally started this silly rumour, and adding quite loudly, "That ruddy cat should stay at the top of the street where she's supposed to live!"

He seemed well cross.

P.S. It didn't hurt when Silly Billy smacked our heads together. Meg's head is so furry; it was like being hit with a cushion!

P.P.S. Who's Henrietta?

Sunday 18 November

Slept really well last night and feel so relaxed today.

It's so good to know that the hobgoblin has left Scary Alley and is never coming back.

My human bought me a new catnip mousie. I played with it for a while. I enjoyed ripping its tail off and it made me dribble happily and lounge on my back, but I like my old catnip mousie the best. It's like a pair of comfy slippers and it really smells disgusting after all my dribbling.

Met Brandy on my favourite shed. I told him to piss off and he told me to piss off back and then we relaxed together. We did a bit of head rubbing and then settled down to a little purring.

Silly Billy came to join us and we spied on big man gardener who came to do the garden. After a while, big man gardener shouted, "Right Rupert, that's your garden put to bed until the spring. Now all I've got to do is put your human to bed until the spring." And then he chuckled.

Silly Billy was not impressed and said that I should

get rid of the bounder. I don't know what he means, but he told me to piddle on big man gardener's clothes and be sick in his shoes and wake him up when he's asleep. I don't think he likes big man gardener. Then we all pissed off because the raining time came.

P.S. My human smelt of dry white wine and roasted pig. So did big man gardener, who spent all day and night with my human.

P.P.S. Jumped on my human's bed and stuck one claw up big man gardener's snout just as he started snoring. It made his eyes water, and then Meg slept on his head again.

Monday 19 November

Had beef for any old cats for my breakfast. I love beef for any old cats.

My human went off to work sulking again, as usual, but she still kissed and cuddled me. She said she loved me dearly. Thank God for that!

Decided to tell all the cats that the hobgoblin had left Scary Alley. I didn't tell Cheese. Instead, I shouted to him across the rusty old car monster, "Oi! Cheese! The hobgoblin's staying in Scary Alley until he's eaten you!"

Cheese ran away.

Ha ha ha!

Tuesday 20 November

Had a relaxing day on the Surrey sofas.

Meg spent most of the day under the bed in her secret

den, coughing up a furball. I felt one coming on too, so I did mine on the kitchen mat.

My human did a lot of huffing and puffing when she came home. I don't know why.

P.S. She spent ages doing her markings with her coloured pens all over the books, and did even more huffing and puffing. She likes a good bit of huffing and puffing. She's just like me!

Wednesday 21 November

Meg came with me to Scary Alley when all the humans were sleeping.

We met Silly Billy, Pickle, Mojo, Jenny, Brandy, and Paddy cat there.

Paddy cat looked well scared when he saw me. He backed away, low-bellied with his eyes looking at the ground, not daring to look at me. I moved towards him in a dominating way, uttering a low menacing growl, with my ears flat. Then Jenny smacked me one and told me not to be so mean to a poor nearly orphaned boy. I still did a bit of tail sniffing with Paddy cat and then I licked his head and left him alone in case Jenny smacked me one again.

We then just sat about catching bugs, spraying up the bins, and doing a bit of yowling all together.

We had a good time, except for Silly Billy who said he was bored and was going off to watch *The Open University*. I asked him what was *The Open University* and he said in a short-tempered way that it was on the television, and so I just told him, quite casually, that there was nothing on our telly cos it's too thin to sit on and then he smacked me one and went off muttering up by the big garages.

Jenny said, "Rupert, *The Open University* is like chess, only harder."

So I smacked her one before she smacked me one again. She went off muttering up by the big garages.

Bloody stupid animals!

Thursday 22 November

My human gave Meg some milk today.

She lapped it up, but I don't think she drank any. It was all over her mouth, nose, and whiskers. She looked ridiculous, so I said, "You look very pretty today, Meg. Why don't you go out and get a boyfriend?"

She said, "Thank you, Rupert, I think I will."

And then she shook her head and the milk splattered all over the floor. For God's sake, she's so dim!

Our human laughed and scooped her up and cuddled her and washed her face. This made Meg cry as usual, so our human kissed her some more. Poor Meg!

P.S. My human went out and came back smelling of roasted beef and far too many glasses of dry white wine. Her eyes looked very peculiar. So did big man gardener's. They crawled up the stairs and shut the bedroom door. I heard a few squeaks and then a lot of snoring. Meg cried and cried until our human let her into the room to sleep on big man gardener's head. Then he woke up and started sneezing again.

Ha ha ha!

Friday 23 November

My human drank loads of glasses of water this morning.

She looked well pissed off when she saw that I'd been sick in big man gardener's shoe. Meg's right: it is just the right size for furball and sick!

My human was huffing and puffing all over the place, but still managed to give me cod and plaice for any old cats for my breakfast. I love cod and plaice for any old cats.

Stayed in all day. I had a big groomin' time and then accidentally coughed up a very big furball on the Surrey sofas. I thought that my human was going to do a lot of huffing and puffing about that furball on the Surrey sofas.

Meg came in and said, "Our human's going to do a lot of huffing and puffing about that furball on the Surrey sofas, Rupert."

When my human came home, she did a lot of huffing and puffing about the furball on the Surrey sofas.

She said, "For God's sake, Meg, why did you have to do a furball on the brand new sofas?"

Ha ha ha!

Saturday 24 November

My human wouldn't get up this morning, but I didn't bite her snout or cough up a furball.

I let her relax, like a cat, and we did some cuddling and purring. She was in a good mood when she got up.

After the biscuit game – which I won 6–0! – she went out hunting and came back and filled up my cat cupboard with food. I spent all day thinking about my cat cupboard. It made me do lots of purring.

Met Silly Billy in the evening. He said, "I'm sorry I smacked you one, Rupert."

I said, "That's all right. Is *The Open University* still on your telly?"

He said, "It's in my television, Rupert. It's in the television. I watch it. I look and listen. It is my window on the world and I love it."

I said, "Is that where you learn to speak dogs' dribble?"

He said, "Yes."

I said, "Well, don't watch it then, you stupid animal!"

For God's sake! Why am I surrounded by dim cats?

Sunday 25 November

Met Pickle today by the sheds.

He said that Cheese had found out that I lied about the hobgoblin. He says that when he sees me, he's going to smack me once, twice, and three times. I ran up my stairs and hid under the bed in Meg's secret den.

P.S. I'm feeling stressed.

P.P.S. I'm feeling hysterical.

Monday 26 November

That bloody cat, Cheese!

He ambushed me by the birch tree in my garden. He

smacked me once, twice, and three times. I hit my chin on the wall and there was blood everywhere.

Cheese said, "You tell me porcupines again and I'll rip yer ears off!" He went off growling.

I hate that Cheese. He's wilder than the wildest animal. He's more vicious than a vicious hobgoblin. He's darker than the darkest night.

When my human saw me, she was quite stressed; in fact, she was hysterical. I tried to pretend there was nothing wrong with me in case she took me to see Mr Muppet.

P.S. My human took me to see Mr Muppet and he put a needle in my fur. Dammit!

P.P.S. If I had one wish, I'd wish that a big hobgoblin would eat Cheese very, very slowly over several days.

P.P.P.S. This is the worst day of my life! What's more, big man gardener stayed the night with my human. Dammit again!

Tuesday 27 November

Spent the day under the bed in Meg's secret den.

Meg and Pickle came to see me and we all licked my wounds.

Pickle apologised for Cheese's behaviour. He explained that he tries to teach him some manners, but Cheese just smacks him once, twice, and three times too. I asked if he takes after his mother.

Pickle said, "I think so. After I'd been up her bottom, she smacked me once, twice, and three times."

Meg said, "All girl cats smack the boys once, twice,

and three times after they've been up their bottoms. It's just a girl thing."

I said, "Why do they do that then?"

Meg said, "I don't know!"

We all decided to have a big sleep cos we were fed up with being cats.

Wednesday 28 November

Feeling better today and there is no sign of a bottom boil.

Ate some beef for senior cats. I love beef for senior cats!

Meg left her turkey and ham for any old cats, so I ate that too.

My human told me off. She said that I was a naughty boy and that I'd get too fat. Stupid human! A fat cat is a happy cat.

Spent the evening in the garden, flicking stones and running up the trees. Meg came to see me with a frog in her mouth. It was wriggling a bit.

She said, "Ook Uper. I gock a og. I oing oo ive it oo ig an argener a a ehun."

I think she was trying to say that she was going to give the frog to big man gardener as a present. I said that was a very good idea and we both ran into our house. Big man gardener was sleeping with our human, in her bed, and Meg put the frog on his head. I don't think either of them appreciated Meg's thoughtfulness.

P.S. I didn't know big man gardener could scream like a big girl.

Thursday 29 November

My human went out hunting for cat food again today.

She caught an enormous box of cat biscuits and two new flea collars. I like my new flea collar. It's soft and fluffy. My human said I look like a royal cat, whatever that may be. Meg went hysterical in her new collar. She ran all over the house shouting, "Rupert, our human's put a flea collar on me. Quick get them off me! I don't want fleas on me!"

I shouted, "You stupid cat! A flea collar's not full of fleas. It stops fleas getting on your fur!"

She said, "I know that!"

As if!

Friday 30 November

It did a lot of raining time today.

Me and Meg went out in our back garden and got our slippered paws all wet and muddy. We decided to decorate the kitchen floor and made mud patterns all over it. When our human came home, she didn't appreciate our work. She just washed it all off, so Meg decided to be sick on the stairs. Our human didn't appreciate that either!

Our human lay on the Surrey sofas all evening. We did a lot of cuddling and purring and dribbling with her. We all had a nice time.

P.S. No sign of big man gardener. Good!

DECEMBER

**Boyfriend trouble all around,
but I love Christmas!**

Saturday 1 December

Ate cod and plaice for any old cats for my breakfast. I love cod and plaice for any old cats.

Found Meg's breakfast. It was upstairs, hidden on the bedroom chest, so I knocked it on the floor and ate that too. My human pretended to growl at me like a wild animal. I went huffing and puffing down my garden. If she growls at me again, I'm going to smack her one.

Spent the evening in the garden with Meg. It was lit by the moon which was big and bright.

I said to Meg, "I wonder why the moon is so big and bright tonight."

She said, "It's because the sun's rays are shining on the whole face of the moon, but it also has a dark side too. It is not a natural light source you know, it—"

I interrupted with, "Meg, have you been talking to Silly Billy?"

She said, "Yes."

I said, "Meg, have you been watching *The Open University* with Silly Billy?"

She said, "Yes."

I said, "Meg, do you want to talk dogs' dribble all your life?"

She said, "No."

I said, "Meg, don't you think you had better stop watching *The Open University*?"

She said, "Yes."

I said, "Meg, I wonder why the moon's so big and bright."

She said, "I don't know!"

Thank God for that!

P.S. We both crept home and went to sleep with our human who was sleeping with big man gardener! Meg slept on his head, and I clawed at his trousers and bottom-sprayed over his coat. Serves him right.

Sunday 2 December

My human got up early and washed the big man gardener's coat with some flowery-smelling stuff and then fed the three of us. Bloody Paddy cat!

Decided to snooze and sulk all day on the Surrey sofas. Kept one eye on my human, but she seems to have given up growling like a wild animal. Thank God!

Went out in the evening and met Mojo and Meg in Mojo's garden. They said I couldn't sit with them because they were having a pedigree evening together.

I went off huffing and puffing to the rusty old car monster and found Jenny sitting there quietly, on her own. I told her about Mojo and Meg and she said not to worry about it; although pedigrees often felt superior to domestic moggies, their gene pool was rather limited and this often led to a distinct lack of brain cells, which was not an attractive feature in any animal.

Silly Billy turned up too and said that education, not breeding, was the key to a better future for all cats and that, one day, this may lead to a seat in Parliament or at the very least, one on the board of the RSPCA.

I didn't know what either of them was talking about so I just said quite casually that I thought I might be a pedigree, anyway, seeing as really I was a Norwegian Forest cat, and Jenny said, "Well then Rupert, that explains everything." And then they both buggered off, chuckling to themselves.

P.S. Big man gardener stayed all day in my house – AGAIN!

Monday 3 December

Nothing much happened today.

Played the biscuit game with my human and won 5–0! Then went on my favourite shed and met Brandy.

I told him to piss off, and he said that Peggy the great snouted barking mad dog had gone. I shouted at him that that was not what I wanted to hear and so he kindly told me to piss off and I thanked him and told him that that was better.

P.S. I'm a bit worried about Peggy the great snouted barking mad dog. Where has she gone?

Tuesday 4 December

Saw Silly Billy by the rusty old car monster.

I asked him where Peggy the great snouted barking mad dog had gone.

He said, "To some heavenly place for great snouted barking mad dogs."

I said, "Where's that then?"

He said, "To some place beyond the realms of cat comprehension, but no doubt she has traversed the rainbow bridge and is now surrounded by positive vibrant vibes."

I said, "What does that mean?"

He said, "You'll not see her again, but I think she's quite happy. She certainly doesn't want us felines to fret for her."

I said, "Is she OK then?"

He said, "Yes."

I said, "Will her human get another great snouted barking mad dog?"

He said, "Quite possibly."

I said, "Good, cos I will miss hearing her barking mad barks."

Silly Billy said he would too. Us cats don't like dogs with their big teeth and snouts, but I'll miss Peggy. She made me go huffing and puffing about my garden and I enjoy a good bit of huffing and puffing.

P.S. Did some more huffing and puffing when I found big man gardener in my human's bed!

Wednesday 5 December

It was storming time today.

I decided to stay in my house in case the wind got up my tail and made me accidentally get stuck up a tree.

Pickle joined me for a snooze on the Surrey sofas.

He's decided to live in our house when my human's not around to kiss him.

Went for a stroll in the evening. It was crisp and starry. Found Silly Billy and Jenny in the potting shed that belongs to the old man with the garden full of summer roses. They were lounging about with their serious faces on, listening to an old radio. They'd be far more relaxed and attractive without their serious faces. I asked them what they were doing and they said that they were listening to a rather good adaptation of Jane Austen's *Persuasion* on Radio 4. Give me strength! I quickly bit their tails and ran away about my cat business.

P.S. I wonder how all those humans get inside that little radio.

P.P.S. I wish I hadn't bitten Jenny's tail. I forgot that I fancy her.

Thursday 6 December

Was up on my favourite shed early this morning, straight after I'd eaten my chicken for senior cats.

I love chicken for senior cats. I love any old meat for any old cats too. In fact, I love eating. I'd die if I couldn't eat!

Eventually, I spotted Jenny in Mojo's garden doing her business very neatly. She buries it thoroughly.

I went to greet her and said, "Jenny, I'm so sorry I bit your tail."

She said, "That's all right, Rupert. Silly Billy and I understand how frustrating it must be to be as dim-witted as you. Indeed, you'll never be able to appreciate the elegant words and finely crafted stories of Jane Austen."

I didn't know what she was dribbling on about, so I just said, "Yes, thank you, Jenny."

I think she was quite impressed.

Friday 7 December

Weather's getting really cold.

The sun is shining and there is no sky blanket to keep us warm. Pickle can't bear it. He's living under our dining room table every minute of the day when my human's not around.

Meg's fur coat is so huge that she keeps having hot flushes. She keeps talking to everyone she meets by the sheds saying that she thinks the summer's coming! She'll never be normal.

P.S. Big man gardener slept in our human's bed. At least it was warm with the four of us.

Saturday 8 December

Had posh rabbit for any old cats today. I love posh rabbit for any old cats.

Met a new cat by the big garages. Her name is Henrietta. She must be the one Silly Billy was muttering about. I think he said that she lives at the top of the street. She's not a middle-of-the-street cat. I've never actually seen her before. She's very skinny, with very short sandy fur and big ears that swivel about like

Mojo's. She must hear everything from the top, to the middle, to the bottom of the street! And she's tall. I think she must be a pedigree cat. She doesn't look one bit like the rest of us. She kept yowling in a deep husky voice.

I said, "Why are you yowling in a deep husky voice? It's not night time."

She yowled some more and said, "I can't help it. I'm an Abyssinian."

I said, "What does that mean?"

She said, "I think I come from Africa and they do yowling in Africa."

I said, "What's Africa?"

She said, "I don't know," and carried on yowling until Meg turned up, and then Henrietta ran away yowling. Meg was well chuffed. She thinks she's well scary with all her fur. I suggested she went and found Cheese and smacked him one.

Meg came home later, crying. She'd found Cheese by Brandy's shed, so she charged at him with all her fur flying. He boxed her ears and smacked her up the bottom, hissing, "Piss off you little rat cat. Yer all fur an' 'ot air!"

Apparently, Brandy piped up, "Piss off yourself," and got his ears boxed too. Cheese has no respect for great and elderly cats, like Brandy. He has no respect for anything! Poor Meg, poor Brandy.

P.S. Actually, the way she farts, Meg is all fur and hot air, but I didn't tell her that.

Sunday 9 December

Ate all my breakfast today.

It was game and turkey for any old cats. Still love game and turkey for any old cats, but I was well sick all over the hall carpet. My human cleared it up and cuddled me to make me feel better. Good job it wasn't the Surrey sofas. Anyway, it's her fault. All my meat should be for senior cats. I think she's getting careless because she keeps spending too much time with big man gardener.

It's just like Brandy said it would be. If she does have a human baby, she might forget to feed me altogether! I really would just die if that happened.

Meg whinged all day. When she's not having a hot flush, she's demanding a new fur coat.

She says, "I want black – no, tortoiseshell – no, white – no, British blue – no, Russian blue with a hint of lavender and medium-length fur – no, short sleek shiny fur – no, long thick greyish bluey-pinky fur to keep me beautifully warm as long as my bum's not too big in it."

I shouted, "Meg, you've already got long thick greyish bluey-pinky fur to keep you warm, even if your bum's a little big in it!"

She said, "Oh yeah! I knew I was gorgeous!" and then ran outside to find herself a boyfriend. Thank God for that!

P.S. My human gave me chicken for senior cats for my tea. Maybe she does still love me. Thank God for that too!

Monday 10 December

Had some more chicken for senior cats for my breakfast.

I love chicken for senior cats, but still felt a little queasy, so I went outside for some fresh air.

The air was very fresh. In fact, it was bloody freezing, even for a Norwegian Forest cat, so I came home and slept in Meg's secret den.

Pickle joined me. We had a nice time until Meg came home all wide-eyed and breathless.

She said she'd just met a lovely new boyfriend in Scary Alley. I asked her what his name was and she said Henrietta.

I said, "For God's sake, Meg, she's a girl!"

She said, "Oh no, he's got a lovely deep throaty yowl."

I said, "That's cos she's from Africa!"

Meg said, "What's Africa?"

I said, "I don't know, but she's definitely a girl."

Pickle said, "Yes, she's definitely a girl."

Meg said, "How do you know?"

Pickle explained that he went out with her for an hour last Friday.

Meg started to cry and so Pickle suggested that he would be quite happy to be her boyfriend again for about three hours. She was quite pleased about this and then we all went sleeping for about three hours.

P.S. Wish my human would only go out with big man gardener for about three hours instead of FOREVER!

Tuesday 11 December

Heard this terrible noise this morning.

It was coming from Scary Alley. It sounded like a creature being slowly eaten alive, so I peeped over the dustbins and discovered it was Henrietta yowling. I jumped on the wall next to her and asked her why she was yowling again. She told me that she was yowling for her new boyfriend, so I asked who that was.

She said, "That great big fluffy grey cat that frightened me the other day, but is really a lovely boy called Meg."

Give me strength!

I boxed her ears and shouted, "That's my little housemate sister and she's a girl!"

Then I went huffing and puffing all the way home.

Wednesday 12 December

Me and Meg decided to find Henrietta.

We wanted to sort out who was the boyfriend and who was the girlfriend, once and for all.

Henrietta was yowling as usual in Scary Alley.

Meg asked her if she was a boy cat, and she said that she wasn't. Meg then said that she looked like a boy, walked like a boy, and yowled like a boy.

Henrietta said, "I'm a girl!"

So I asked her if she would consider going up a girl's bottom.

Henrietta said, "What with?"

Me and Meg said, "She's a girl."

And then Henrietta said that of course she was a girl and accused Meg of being the boy with her monster fur coat! Meg said, "I'm a pedigree Persian princess. Look at my cute nose, wide eyes, and pouting lips. I'm so pretty, I must be a girl!"

And so I asked Meg if she would consider going up a girl's bottom.

She said, "What with?"

Me and Henrietta said, "She's definitely a girl."

Then Meg and Henrietta said, "Well, who's the boy then?"

And I said, "I am."

And then they asked if I would go out with them, seeing as I was the boy and I said, "No!"

We were exhausted after all this thinking, so we all swished our tails, having confused ourselves, and then went home for a snooze.

P.S. Henrietta lives at the top of the street. Scary Alley is for the middle-of-the-street cats. She's not allowed in our middle-street territory! Tomorrow, I'm going to tell her to piss off back to the top of the street.

P.P.S. My human forgot to do any markings with her pens in her books because she was too busy kissing and cuddling big man gardener on the Surrey sofas. Her markings are going from shoddy to non-existent! Disgusting behaviour!

Thursday 13 December

Breakfast was delicious!

Had really posh chicken and liver for any old cats. I

scoffed it down and then was sick all over the back door mat. Set off for Scary Alley as soon as I'd been sick.

Silly Billy was already there talking to Henrietta.

He said, "I'm sorry, Henrietta, but you can't possibly stay a minute longer. Your yowling is unspeakably irritating, you can't play chess, and this alley is beyond the boundaries of your own top-of-the-street territory."

Henrietta did some more yowling and started to cry, but Silly Billy just said, "You must go, before you upset the delicate balance of the minds of the middle-street cats. If that happens, all manner of yowling, spitting, and fighting will break out."

Henrietta kept on yowling and crying and said that she didn't want to go back to the top of the street because a big dog named Floyd lived there and he was really scary.

Silly Billy just said that Cheese was worse than the big dog Floyd and he was going to tear her to pieces any minute now.

With that, Henrietta ran like a great snouted barking mad dog, with big legs, all the way to the top of the street!

P.S. My human came home, without the big man gardener, smelling of two halves of lager and pork roasted in wine. She cleared up the sick. I did cuddling with her all night. We both loved it!

Friday 14 December

Woke up feeling well scared.

What if Cheese decides to tear me to shreds now that

Henrietta has left the middle-of-the-street territory?

I hid under the bed in Meg's secret den all day. So did Pickle and Meg. We had two reasons for doing this: one, we're scared; two, it's bloody freezing. Even Meg's bottom has been penetrated, but only by the cold.

P.S. Really scared today.

P.P.S. It's really bloody cold today.

P.P.P.S. It's really bloody freezing today. All four of us spent the night in human's bed. It kept us warm again, and at least no bottom fiddling!

Saturday 15 December

The whole world is frosted this morning.

My slippered paws were freezing on the crunchy ground, but I was determined to speak to Silly Billy, so I went to the rusty old car monster and started calling for him. He soon came.

He was very cross and said, "Rupert, why are you yowling for me? On a day like this, you should be at home with your human who loves you."

I said, "Well that's all very well, Silly Billy, but since you've got rid of Henrietta, Cheese may well be after a middle-of-the-street cat now. He may well tear me to pieces instead of her. I think you should get Henrietta back so that Cheese can tear her to pieces instead of me."

Silly Billy said, "I'm so sorry, Rupert. My porcupine was to Henrietta, not you. I made up the story of Cheese tearing her to pieces to get rid of her. Believe me, Cheese may well give you a bottom boil, but he has no reason to tear any of the middle-of-the-street cats to pieces, now that order has been restored to our territory."

I said, "Are you sure?"

He said, "Of course I'm sure. It's crisp and cold and time for Christmas. Yes, Christmas is coming! Can't you see it in the lighted houses? Is your human not frantically buying presents and putting up cards and decorations?"

I said, "That word 'Christmas' does ring a jingle bell, Silly Billy, but I can't remember a thing about it."

Silly Billy said, "Well, you go home and try to have a think, Rupert. In fact, spend the whole day having a big think. It'll do you good."

So I went home and I did.

Sunday 16 December

I remember Christmas!

My human stayed home and put up lots of cards today. Then she put up a big tree. It's all shiny and lighted with little lights. She said that I could help to decorate the tree with her, so I flicked a few bows and tore at the angels, and she laughed. She's easily pleased.

She said that she was going to put my Christmas present under the tree, and she asked me what I would like. I thought that I'd like a catnip mousie and lots of cat biscuit treats, and then she said, "I'm going to buy you a catnip mousie and lots of cat biscuit treats." She buys me that every year.

P.S. I like Christmas.

P.P.S. I like my human too.

Monday 17 December

Still crisp and cold.

Played races down the stairs and the biscuit game with my human. I won 7–0!

Then I sat all day on the Surrey sofas looking at the Christmas tree. Felt the urge to flick a few decorations around the room.

Pickle wouldn't play with me. He slept in Meg's secret den.

Meg wouldn't play with me. She went out to find another boyfriend. Typical!

My human came home with my presents. She's put them in my cat cupboard for now.

Then Meg came home all wide-eyed and breathless saying she's going out with the rabbit that lives in the garden opposite us! Give me strength!

Tuesday 18 December

Had tuna for senior cats for my breakfast. I love tuna for senior cats.

Wanted to eat Meg's breakfast, but my human hid it from me. This put me in a bad mood so I smacked Meg onc. How dare she go out with a rabbit!

I said to her, "How dare you go out with a rabbit!"

She said, "Actually, I'm going out with two and they're called Lupin and Rodney."

I asked if Lupin was a girl. She said that she didn't know, she didn't care, and that they were both gorgeous with white fluffy fur and that they ate carrots.

I said that I hoped the fierce foxy would eat them! She smacked me one and went huffing and puffing down the garden.

My human came home and wrapped my presents and put them under the Christmas tree.

I can smell the biscuits and the catnip mousie, but I won't tear them open with my sharp claws. My human likes to open them for me on Christmas morning. She gets so excited, so I won't spoil her fun.

Me and my human did cuddling and dribbling in the evening. We had a nice time without big man gardener. Good!

Wednesday 19 December

Met Brandy on my favourite shed today.

We huddled together because it was quite cold. I asked him what he was getting for Christmas. He said that he was getting a catnip mousie and some cat treat biscuits. I said that so was I. We did some good purring together.

Silly Billy joined us for a huddle. I asked him what he would like for Christmas. He said, "I'd like a scholarship to read Latin, applied mathematics, and eighteenth-century Norwegian philosophy at Oxford, but I expect I'll have to put up with a catnip mouse and some cat treat biscuits." Then he went huffing and puffing down the garden, and me and Brandy pissed off for a piddle.

Went home to cuddle my human. She was wrapping up a big present.

She put it under the tree and said, "Look Rupert, this is for the big man gardener. It's a rather lovely – and expensive – cashmere jumper to keep him warm in the gardens. He's coming for Christmas!"

She left the room and I accidentally tore at the paper. Actually, I tore the paper to shreds.

P.S. Felt just like Cheese cat.

P.P.S. My human was well cross with me. I don't know why. My tearing of paper usually makes her laugh.

Thursday 20 December

Had rabbit for senior cats for my breakfast. I love rabbit for senior cats.

I told Meg, but she wasn't very pleased. She said that she hoped I hadn't eaten her boyfriends, and I said that my food tasted a bit like Lupin mixed up with Rodney.

She raced out the cat flap and down the garden. I've never seen her huff and puff so much.

I did some lounging by the Christmas tree with Pickle. We had a nice time, but as soon as my human came home, Pickle ran away with a look of blind terror on his face. I don't know why. She's only a little bit ugly and she never smacks us cats one. She just kisses us and cuddles us and kisses us.

Spent the evening with my human. She wrapped some more presents, and I ate some wrapping paper and a few angels, which seemed to amuse her.

Accidentally got my paws wrapped in the sticky tape. This did not amuse me, but needless to say, it did seem to amuse my human. The only thing that doesn't seem to amuse her is me tearing at big man gardener's present.

She's hidden that from me. Dammit!

Friday 21 December

Stayed in all day and so did Meg.

It was far too cold to go outside, and Meg couldn't play with her boyfriends because they stayed deep in their hutch.

My human got all dressed up in the evening in what she called her 'best posh frock'. I could tell she was pleased with herself, but she'll never be gorgeous. How can she be, with that great snout and furless skin? Disgusting!

Big man gardener came to call for her. When he saw her, he said she looked lovely. I didn't know humans told porcupines too. I thought that was a cat thing.

My human came home smelling of roasted bird and trillions of glasses of dry white wine, but at least she didn't fall over, except into bed with big man gardener. He didn't stay long though. He had a terrible sneezing fit when Meg slept on his head. Then he got up and was sick all over the bathroom floor. Then he left.

P.S. I didn't know humans could be sick all over the bathroom floor too. I thought that was a cat thing.

Saturday 22 December

My human was well cross, this morning, and spent a lot of time cleaning the bathroom.

She did feed me turkey for senior cats. I love turkey for senior cats, but she wouldn't play the biscuit game with me. She just kept muttering about big man gardener.

Us cats met in Scary Alley. Silly Billy said that he wanted to educate us about some Christmas traditions.

We didn't really know what he was talking about, but we were quite worried when he told us that some great red-nosed snouted animal flew through the sky carrying presents to children. We're not too sure about great snouted animals. Some of us are not too sure about children!

Meg sneaked off to see her boyfriends in their rabbit hutch, but she soon came back to Scary Alley all wide-eyed and breathless. She started to cry and told us that she'd gone to the hutch and saw Rodney up Lupin's bottom and she didn't think that was very nice.

Mojo said, "Poor Meg's been two-timed by Lupin!"

And Jenny said, "And poor Meg's been two-timed by Rodney."

And Silly Billy said, "Now there's a problem. Has Meg been two-timed twice to make four-timed, or has she been two-timed squared?"

We all said, "We don't know!"

And Silly Billy said, "Neither do I, but with a degree in applied mathematics, maybe I would!"

Everyone got confused, so we all went home worried about snouted animals, except for Silly Billy who went home muttering about the deeper implications of applied mathematics, whatever that means.

P.S. It's such a shame that Silly Billy's head is full of dogs' dribble.

P.P.S. Lovely time sleeping on the bed, kissing and cuddling our human. Just the three of us and no sign of big man gardener. Ha ha ha!

Sunday 23 December

My human keeps showing me my present that's under the Christmas tree.

She said about five times, "Look Rupert, this is your present. It's a catnip mousie and your favourite cat treat biscuits." I know that, but when do we open them?

We all met Silly Billy in Scary Alley again. He told us that we open our presents soon, on Christmas Day. I was pleased about that. I was just about to ask him when Christmas Day was when we all heard a terrible hissing and growling from behind the dustbins. We all yelled "Cheese!" and scarpered, in case he tore us to pieces.

P.S. Meg found a dead mousie in our garden and took it home for the big man gardener. He was in our human's bed, as usual, and so Meg dropped it very carefully on his head. He screamed like a big girl, again, and shouted, "Those bloody cats! I've had enough!" And then he cleared off to his own home. Ha ha ha!

Monday 24 December

Meg found Lupin and Rodney hopping about their garden so she smacked them one and pulled out their fur.

I watched her from my favourite shed. She was well cross.

She shouted, "I'm never being four-timed or two-timed squared ever again by a couple of carrot-eating cretinous creatures!"

They shouted that she was worse than a foxy, and she shouted, "Good! And if you don't get in your hutch, I'll eat you raw!" So they did.

She came huffing and puffing onto my favourite shed.

I said, "Well done, Meg. What does cretinous mean?"

She said, "I don't know. Silly Billy told me to say it."

Me and Pickle and Brandy met Silly Billy in Scary Alley again for our next bit of Christmas education. He told us about a baby human born in a stable surrounded by animals, except for cats.

Brandy said, in a rather bitter voice, that if there were no cats then they could all piss off and take the human baby with them!

Silly Billy tried to explain that cats weren't exactly banned when suddenly Meg appeared all wide-eyed and breathless, and shouted, "That great red-nosed snouted animal has got stuck in the window over the way! He can't get out!"

Pickle said that there would be no presents tonight for the children, and Silly Billy fell on his back laughing and said, "That particular great red-snouted creature is just a collection of flickering lights put there by the humans," and then he added, "And anyway, the story of Father Christmas and Rudolph the red-nosed reindeer is just a legend brought forth each year to symbolise the spirit of giving, which is indicative of the Christmas season; hence all this present buying, even for cats!"

We were all confused as usual, but we've given up smacking him one. Instead, we all went off together to look at the lighted windows. We counted six Rudolphs, nine Father Christmases, and five snowmen in the middle-of-the-street houses. We had a good time.

P.S. Three of us in the bed tonight.

P.P.S. Our human cuddled me and Meg all night. No big man gardener. Happy cat Rupert!

Tuesday 25 December

I think Christmas has come.

My human gave me and Meg chicken and turkey for any old cats. I love chicken and turkey for any old cats.

Then she went out the front and gave Paddy chicken and turkey for any old cats – annoying little beggar of an animal.

My human then got really excited and carried me to the Christmas tree and opened my present. It was a catnip mousie and some cat treat biscuits! I ate lots of cat treat biscuits. They tasted of beef. I love cat treat biscuits that taste of beef!

Meg got a catnip mousie and some cat treat biscuits from the human too. We played with our catnip mousies. I flicked mine about and sniffed it and bit it and licked it. I loved the smell of it. I found myself lying on my back, stretching out my legs, and feeling dead cool and relaxed. I did a lot of dribbling too. So did Meg.

My human invited some of her human relatives to my house. And then the big man gardener turned up. Dammit!

She did lots of cooking, but she didn't look too pleased. Big man gardener had said he was sorry about not getting her favourite perfume, but his work was seasonal and he couldn't afford much at this time of the year. My human was not impressed. She just banged some pots on the kitchen surface and drank some wine.

Big man gardener sat on the Surrey sofas, drinking beer and eating a selection of dates, nuts, and crisps. Meg decided to flirt with him and sat all over his lap and neck and head.

He started sneezing and crying and then he leapt up off the Surrey sofa and shouted, "That's it! I've had enough of these stupid spoilt pathetic cats. You need to put them OUTSIDE!"

Poor Meg fell off his neck and scarpered straight out the cat flap. I was so shocked at big man gardener shouting that I scarpered too.

Me and Meg ran out of the garden and onto the rusty old car monster. Then Meg had to jump off for a quick unexpected piddle. We couldn't believe a human could be so scary! Our human talks to us as though we are still little kittens, all soft and gentle. We licked each other's ears and wondered what to do.

We were soon joined by Brandy, complaining that his house was full of noisy human grandchildren who kept shrieking and pulling his tail.

Little Mojo soon turned up; shocked that her human had drunk so much sherry that she kept falling over.

Then Silly Billy and Jenny turned up saying they were disappointed with their poxy old catnip Christmas mousies and had played with them, for the benefit of the humans, for long enough.

Me and Meg told them that we loved our catnip mousies.

Silly Billy said he objected to being turned into a drug addict by his thoughtless humans. Then, we sat about a bit together talking about how nasty big man gardener was.

It was cold, even in our fur, but none of us wanted to go home until Paddy, of all cats, turned up and begged us to get our humans to save him some pig sausages in little duvets.

We'd thought he'd gone mad, except for Brandy who exclaimed, "Oh yes, it's great big roasting bird day with all the trimmings!"

And then we all started sniffing the air and indeed, great big roasting birds with all the trimmings came wafting from all the kitchens of the middle-of-the-street territory.

"Well done, Brandy! You are indeed right!" said Silly Billy.

With that, we all scarpered back to our homes, with the sounds of Paddy's, "Don't forget my pig sausages in little duvets," filling the gardens as we ran.

When we got back to our house, I pushed Meg through the cat flap first and when she didn't explode back out again, I made my way into the kitchen too.

Our human was crying and asking who would mow the lawn and prune the roses in the spring now? The other humans were soothing her and feeding her Prosecco and there was no sign of big man gardener! Then when she saw us, she picked us up and cuddled and kissed us.

She said, "I'm so sorry about big man gardener, my darlings. He was so horrid to you, and he said to me that I would rather sleep with a spoilt Persian princess and a fat mummy's boy than with him. And do you know what, my darlings? He's right!"

And then she kissed us and cuddled us some more and everyone laughed.

The rest of the day was well good without big man gardener, and all the humans had a lovely time eating big roasting bird with all the trimmings, and me and Meg had a lovely time eating big roasting bird and all the trimmings too. Then the humans settled down and had a good day, laughing, farting and playing games.

Went out later for a piddle and then came home and spent all night cuddling my human.

P.S. My human went out the front in the evening and gave that whining Paddy five pig sausages in little duvets. For God's sake! He always gets his own way.

P.P.S. I think the big man gardener called me a fat cat. Happy cat Rupert!

P.P.P.S. As she cuddled me and Meg, our human told us that big man gardener will never be welcome in our house again. I love Christmas!

Wednesday 26 December

Woke up feeling so happy.

No big man gardener anywhere! My human seemed happy too and did a lot of kissing and cuddling. We played running down the stairs, and the biscuit game. I won 5–0! Then she gave me any old fish and some roasted bird for my breakfast. I love any old fish and roasted bird.

Went out early to take the cool sharp air and met Silly Billy by the rusty old car monster. He asked me if I enjoyed the Queen's speech yesterday.

I said, "What queen?"

He said, "THE QUEEN! MISSIS MA'AM! She spoke to us on the television yesterday. In fact, every year she speaks to us on the television and the humans stop drinking and eating and farting and burping, and listen to her before they fall asleep."

I said, "I've told you before, Silly Billy, she can't fit on our telly cos it's a FLAT SCREEN!"

And then he smacked me one, for God's sake! I was about to smack him one back, but Jenny turned up so I told them both that my human had said that big man gardener was not welcome ever again in our house.

Silly Billy said that it was for the best because he had the feeling, especially after the shouting episode yesterday, that the big man gardener was nothing but a feckless bounder.

Jenny added that she knew my human couldn't really greatly esteem him and that he was indeed a bounder and a cad.

I said, "Thank you very much, Jenny and Silly Billy."

As I left them, Jenny shouted, "You may send my compliments to your human. I am most seriously pleased with her."

As usual, I had no idea what Jenny was going on about, so I quickly ran off and met Pickle in my garden. I invited him to come and flick my Christmas mousie about the living room cos he didn't get any presents. He enjoyed that, and then we spent the rest of the day snoozing with Meg in our secret den under the bed.

My human went out all afternoon and evening and came back smelling of cold roasted turkey and one or two glasses of dry white wine. Meg said that when me and Pickle were snoring, she saw the big man gardener creeping up the stairs to our human's bedroom, even though our human wasn't at home.

P.S. I think Meg must have been having a nightmare or else she's gone completely mad.

P.P.S. The house did have a slight whiff of big man gardener.

P.P.P.S. My human found a tiny box of chocolates under her pillow when we went to bed. She was well cross.

Thursday 27 December

Meg was huffing and puffing all over the house today.

She was sick, on purpose, and she's hidden the Christmas mousies. I asked her what was up and she said that she was cross because she didn't get a new fur coat for Christmas and she hasn't got a boyfriend – not even a rabbit boyfriend – and even our human's boyfriend had left us.

I told Meg that it was a good thing that our human's boyfriend had left us, and with all her lovely fur, she could piss off out into the cold and find a new boyfriend – for her, not our human!

I chased her out the cat flap and she huffed and puffed right out of the garden.

I spent a nice day cuddling my human by the fire. I think she's given up dry white wine today in favour of all her Christmas chocolate, apart from the little box she found under the pillow. She threw that one in the bin. I don't know why.

P.S. Meg came home very late, all full of herself, saying she had been playing chess with Silly Billy. Give me strength!

Friday 28 December

My human hasn't been to work all week, but I think she's allowed to stay at home cos it's Christmas.

We were having a nice snoozing time when she suddenly leapt up and said, "Quick, Rupert, we must get up! My sister's coming to stay."

For God's sake! Her sister's always coming to stay and bringing different big human men with her. I don't want big humans in my house. It's my house. I only let my human stay because she feeds me!

I went huffing and puffing down my garden. Met Silly Billy, but was so cross I smacked him one.

I asked him if he'd been playing chess with Meg.

He said, "I've been playing chess. Meg's been flicking stones about."

I don't know what he means, so I ignored him and went to Mojo's garden to do a bit of yowling with her. I told her I've decided that I'm definitely a pedigree and she seems to like me a lot more now. In fact, I think she looks up to me cos I'm quite mature and very wise, compared to most middle-of-the-street cats.

Then I came home and hid in the secret den under the bed because I'm fed up with humans staying in my house.

P.S. My human's sister and her big man arrived, but at least it's not big man gardener. Ha ha ha!

Saturday 29 December

Decided to ignore all humans today and just eat my breakfast.

I had tuna for senior cats. I love tuna for senior cats.

Meg seemed much happier today and kept flirting with the sister's big man. I asked her very politely where she had hidden our Christmas mousies and she just said, "I don't know!"

Stupid cat!

Listened to my human talking to her sister. She told her that the big man gardener had used his key and crept in the house on Boxing Day and had left a tiny box of chocolates under her pillow. She said she phoned him and thanked him for his tiny box of chocolates, but what she would really like him to do was to return her key and never enter her house again.

She did some giggling with her sister and then she picked me up and kissed me a million times. She told her sister that I was her precious poodle and one true love. I know that.

My human went out with the other humans all evening. Thank God!

Had a relaxing snoozing time without any humans about. They came home very late smelling of dry white wine and chicken korma. It was disgusting!

P.S. When my human returned, she found a key on the doormat. Ha ha ha!

Sunday 30 December

Woke up early and went on a mission to find the Christmas mousies.

They were under the cushions on the Surrey sofas.

Told Meg how stupid she was and she smacked me one, so I smacked her one back and we both went huffing and puffing down the cold crispy garden.

We met Jenny and she told us that Silly Billy said we must all meet in Scary Alley tomorrow night because we were having a party. Me and Meg were so delighted we licked each other's ears and made friends.

Spent the evening cuddling my human on the Surrey sofas. I tried to ignore the sister and her big man but actually, they spoke nicely to me and I loved being in the warm room with the roaring fire and the lighted tree and the humans. I had a good time.

Monday 31 December

Really glad when the evening came and very glad to get out of my house.

My human seemed to have invited all her family and friends over, except big man gardener! Me and Meg legged it before they all started drinking zillions of glasses of dry white wine and accidentally standing on our tails.

Met all the other cats in Scary Alley. To begin with, the evening was a bit scary cos we all heard a low scary yowl. We were just about to scarper when we realised it was only Henrietta, who suddenly appeared on the wall. She was desperate to join our party and we decided that she could, as long as she didn't confuse us all again by going out with Meg.

And then the dustbins began to rattle and the hideous form of...Cheese came into view. We got ready to scarper again when he cried, "I want to come to the party!"

Jenny said, "Cheese, you're welcome to stay, but you must promise not to bite us or frighten us once."

Cheese promised that he wouldn't. He tried hard to make his eyes look normal and keep his ears forward in a friendly manner.

Meg went right up to him and stood face-to-face. She was wide-eyed and breathless, but managed to say, "Cheese, will you be my boyfriend for the night?"

Cheese said, "OK, Meg, but I might smack you one tomorrow."

She said, "OK, but don't give me a bottom boil."

Cheese said, "OK, I'm not as 'orrible as you think."

We all said that he was pretty horrible and we wanted to know why, and Cheese said that he had had a troubled kittenhood. We asked him what had happened and he said that his mother had deserted him as soon as he was on solids.

We said, "All mothers desert their kittens. They get fed up with them. It's the way of all cats!"

Cheese looked amazed.

Pickle said, "I'll always be there for you, son."

With that, Cheese rushed over to Pickle and licked his ears and then Pickle licked Cheese's ears. It was amazing, so we all licked each other's ears and had a great time sitting together, bug flicking, and piddling up dustbins.

Then Henrietta started yowling. It was truly awesome. She'd be a great asset to any cats' choir and we've decided that she can come to all our middle-street parties. We joined her on the wall to do some yowling together when, all of a sudden, all hell broke loose! The sky filled with coloured lights and huge enormous frightening bangs. Every single human in the middle-street neighbourhood came out of their houses to make their own terrible yowling sounds. We all scarpered.

Me and Meg fled back to our house and we were soon under the bed in our secret den. When we looked around, we couldn't believe it! So were Pickle, Paddy, Brandy, Mojo, Jenny, Silly Billy, Henrietta, and Cheese!

We tried to keep calm and play the *Animal, Vegetable, Mineral* game under the bed, but only Silly Billy and

Jenny understood how to play. It all got a little bit confusing with Jenny and Silly Billy talking their complete dogs' dribble!

Eventually, we all did a little bit of snoozing, but as soon as the light came, the other cats crept silently past the wine glasses downstairs and out into the crisp morning air.

We had a good time, us middle-of-the-street cats and Henrietta.

HAPPY NEW YEAR!

Tuesday 1 January

Had posh rabbit and rice for senior cats for my breakfast. I love posh rabbit and rice for senior cats.

My human wanted to play the biscuit game and I won 5–0! She was delighted with me and said she loved me dearly. I know that.

Met Brandy on my favourite shed and he asked me what I wanted to do in this New Year.

I said, "Eat my breakfast, dinner, and supper every day and pinch Meg's breakfast, dinner, and supper every day, because I really love my breakfast, dinner, and supper every day and I really love pinching Meg's breakfast, dinner, and supper every day—"

Brandy said, "SHUT UP, Rupert!"

And then I added that I'd be looking forward to a lot of huffing and puffing and smacking Silly Billy one and being scared down Scary Alley, and most of all, telling him to "PISS OFF!" every day.

That made Brandy really chuckle and so we had a bit of a laugh together and then we both pissed off for a piddle and a snooze.

Spent the evening with my human. She did groomin' all of Meg's fur and we both coped with Meg's farting.

Then me and Meg and my human did some cuddling and dribbling and purring together.

I had a good day.

P.S. I love me.

P.P.S. I love Meg.

P.P.P.S. I love my human too.

Printed in Great Britain
by Amazon